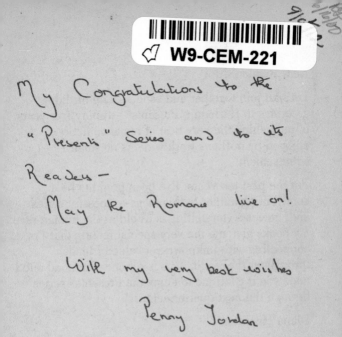

My Congratulations to the

"Presents" Series and to its

Readers —

May the Romance live on!

With my very best wishes

Penny Jordan

Dear Reader,

Let's all join together and send special birthday greetings to Harlequin Presents®—twenty-five years of publishing the very best of romance fiction, enjoyed by millions worldwide, is no small achievement!

For the past ten years, I've been proud to be a contributing author to this mega-successful series and, because storytelling is as old as the human race, my books give me the very special feeling that I'm connecting with unknown yet valued friends throughout the world. This is a wonderful bond and I hope you'll continue to enjoy the Presents® series through the next quarter century!

Diana Hamilton

P.S. *The Millionaire's Baby* is part of a compelling new series, NANNY WANTED!, in which some of our most popular authors create nannies whose talents extend way beyond taking care of the kids!

DIANA HAMILTON

The Millionaire's Baby

Harlequin Books

TORONTO • NEW YORK • LONDON
AMSTERDAM • PARIS • SYDNEY • HAMBURG
STOCKHOLM • ATHENS • TOKYO • MILAN
MADRID • WARSAW • BUDAPEST • AUCKLAND

ISBN 0-373-11956-9

THE MILLIONAIRE'S BABY

First North American Publication 1998.

CHAPTER ONE

CAROLINE FARR was afraid she'd made a terrible mistake.

As the taxi wove through the snarl of traffic on Prince Albert Road she was convinced of it. So utterly convinced she had to grit her teeth in order to stop herself from telling the driver to stop and allow her to walk off her agitation in the sun-drenched greenness of London's Regent's Park.

It was so, so tempting...Mary Greaves, her business partner, could phone through and apologise, explain to the Helliars that, unfortunately, Ms Farr was unable to attend the interview for the position of nanny to their baby daughter, suggest another applicant, another interview.

But she wasn't that weak! Mercifully, the unaccustomed feeling of panic began to subside as the taxi made a left turn into one of the leafy Georgian streets that abounded in this area. She wasn't going to back down at the last moment and prove Mary right. It wasn't in her nature to back away from her own decisions.

Mary had said, 'Caro! Have you gone mad? You can't do it! You're not trained—you know nothing about caring for children! That's my area of expertise, not yours. Think of the agency's reputation!'

And for the first time ever she had pulled rank and reminded her partner of just who had built up that enviable reputation, adding, 'I've worked all hours on the administration side for two whole years. Now I fancy some hands-on experience. Humour me, Mary!' Her smile when she'd wanted to appear relaxed had been big and wide and winning. 'Looking after a child can't be all that difficult. Millions of women do it all the time—and if I get out of my depth I promise I'll let you know. The Grandes Familles Agency is as much my baby as yours; I won't do a thing to harm our good reputation.'

The bit about fancying some hands-on experience had been a downright lie, plucked out of the air as an excuse for what had to appear as sheer craziness, a totally uncharacteristic deviation from her normal level-headed approach to her work at the agency.

But was it so crazy to want revenge?

She'd been in the main office when Honor, their secretary, had shown Finn Helliar into the room Mary used for client interviews. The band that had tightened around her chest with the painful suddenness of a steel trap had kept her immobile until Honor had teetered back on her very high heels a few moments later, a pussy-cat smile on her pretty, pointed face.

Caroline hadn't needed to ask who he was. She'd known. She had never met him but she knew all about him, had seen that photograph in the press a couple of years ago. Handsome as he had looked—his smile tender for the lovely new bride on his arm—the camera image hadn't done him justice. In the flesh his impact was nothing short of stunning.

She'd asked instead, 'Why is he here?' and she'd thanked heaven her voice sounded normal, coolly interested and utterly professional.

'Some hunk, huh?' Honor had smoothed the fabric of her pale grey skirt over her hips. 'He phoned first thing this morning before you arrived. It seems they flew in from Canada a couple of days ago and need a temporary nanny until they find a permanent home outside of London. Nice work for some lucky lady!'

It had been then, precisely then, that Caroline knew what she was going to do, and when Honor had mused, 'I wonder what his wife's like?' she'd merely shaken her head and gone into her own office to wait until her partner had finished interviewing Finn Helliar.

She could have told her secretary exactly who his wife was, what she looked like, but had been afraid she wouldn't be able to hide her anger and outrage if she did.

Now, as the taxi drew up in front of the hotel where the Helliars were staying, Caroline swiftly ran through a mental check-list.

A good nanny was quiet and subdued in her appearance.

Well, she had done her best in that respect.

The mandatory street-wear uniform of the Grandes Familles nannies meant her slim body was successfully de-sexed by the severely plain, tailored dark grey linen suit, the desired touch of white at her throat given by the crisply starched cotton shirt she wore beneath it, her jaw-length bob of glossy, dark auburn hair hidden beneath the grey cloche-style hat, her five feet six inches played down by her sensible flat-heeled shoes.

A good nanny had received rigorous training and carried impeccable references. Caroline Farr had the benefit of neither and as soon as that was discovered she would be shown the door.

Which meant she would have to deliver her castigation right there and then. She would prefer more time to plot a more fitting retribution but only by her acceptance as the Helliars' temporary nanny could she get that.

She would just have to keep her fingers crossed and hope that the gods of retribution were fighting her corner!

After paying off the driver she faced the hotel, straightening. She would have expected Finn Helliar, hot-shot financier, chief executive of an awe-inspiringly successful international merchant bank, to choose something ultra-modern, trendily sophisticated. But maybe his wife had insisted on somewhere like this—restrained, comfortable, old-fashioned, even.

Caroline shrugged. It wasn't important. And the niggle of anxiety she had been trying to suppress bubbled up to the surface of her mind, making her frown and sink her teeth into her full lower lip.

The trouble with knee-jerk reactions, as her impulse to present herself as a temporary nanny had been, was a built-in, fatal lack of forward planning. She was uncomfortable with that.

So far she had planned her life meticulously; she had known where she was going, what she wanted. And if, as was a distinct possibility, she was shown the door as soon as her lack of credentials became known she could only hope that Finn Helliar himself would show her to that door and not leave the chore to his wife.

If the worst came to the worst and she was asked to leave she would say she needed a few moments alone with him. No way would she say what needed to be said in front of his wife. Fleur Helliar wasn't the guilty one.

She stiffly approached the revolving doors with their solid mahogany and brass fittings. It would work out. Fate had obligingly delivered the callous brute into her hands—it wouldn't let her down at this last minute.

The sitting room of the suite she was shown into had all the comfortable, relaxed charm of an English country home and the receptionist she had announced herself to, and who had spoken for a few seconds into the house phone, now said, 'Make yourself comfortable. Mr Helliar asked me to give you his apologies. He won't be more than a few minutes.'

It was, however, much less than that. Just a few seconds, but time enough to note two silver-framed photographs of his wife, the French singer who had briefly blazed to stardom before marriage and imminent motherhood had taken her to apparent obscurity.

His sudden, silent emergence into the room was a shock. It shouldn't have been, but it was. His appearance took her by the throat and shook her, dislodging all her famed composure, depriving her of her wits so that she could only stand and stare at six feet something of honed male power.

His soft dark hair was appealingly rumpled, sticking up in wayward tufts, making him look younger than his thirty-four years. The front of the white shirt he wore above narrow black trousers was decidedly damp, the sleeves rolled up to expose the tanned skin of strong forearms. And his hands, the hands that held the child so gently and held her unwillingly fascinated stare for longer than was sensible, were beautifully made, strong-boned yet sensitive.

'Please excuse the delay, Miss Farr. Sophie got more lunch outside her than in. She and I both agreed—didn't we, my pet?—that she'd look more presentable after a bath, though the same can't be said for me! Won't you sit down?'

The intent silver-grey, black-fringed eyes were bright with enquiry, yet they held a hint of mischief, too. Caroline didn't like that because that, and his rumpled appearance, the loving way he held the baby, made him seem human.

Reminding herself that he wasn't—only a cold-hearted, selfish, inhuman brute could have done what he'd done to her young sister, Katie—she sat, feet neatly together, her features carefully blank.

As the interview progressed, Caroline realised he was more interested in what made her tick, as a person, than in references and credentials. He didn't mention either and she found herself enjoying the experience of re-inventing herself, presenting him with a dedicated lover of children whose hobbies were knitting, making model castles out of matchsticks, collecting wild flowers and recipes for fairy cakes.

The twitching of his mobile, sexy mouth brought her back to reality with a thump. Aborting her flights of fantasy, she asked herself tartly what she thought she was playing at. She should be taking advantage of what fate had handed her and giving him a piece of her mind.

No sign of Fleur, his wife. She wouldn't be out shopping or lunching with friends while something as important as an interview for a nanny was going on.

So she was probably back in her native France, re-cording an album, or whatever pop stars did when they wanted to make a come-back. Nothing had been heard of the singer since her short but meteoric rise to fame had been grounded by marriage and mother-hood. No doubt she was re-launching her career—hence the need for a nanny.

But something held her back—the memory of what he'd done to poor sweet Katie...

Wait and see. If he offered her the job she'd have more time at her disposal to think up something more fitting than a mere tongue-lashing.

As yet she had no idea of what that something might be. But she'd get there. Hadn't her formidable old grandmother repeatedly praised her for being strong and resourceful, a chip off the old Farr block?

'Of course, if you enjoy the situation, if Sophie takes to you, and you don't object to living out of town, then the situation could be permanent.'

It wasn't a statement. More like a question, a prob-ing question at that. Caroline shook her head and did her best to look regretful. No way. No way! This was a one-off. She was no nanny, she was simply the busi-ness brain behind the agency. She wouldn't need long to find a way to pay him back and after that he wouldn't see her for the jet-stream!

'I'm afraid I only ever take temporary work, Mr Helliar.' Earnestly said, with a tiny smile.

'Can you tell me why?' One sable brow slanted towards his hairline, the slight alteration in expression suddenly reminding her that he wasn't the pussy-cat his relaxed pose, with the child perched on his knee, suggested. This was a formidable man.

Pulling an answer out of the air, she invented, 'I get far too fond of my charges if I stay around for longer than a few weeks. It's easier for all concerned if I take on temporary situations only.'

But he didn't believe her. She could see he didn't. The silver eyes had gone hard and flat. She could almost hear the scornful words, calling her a liar, clicking around in his brain.

She knew she'd been telling fibs, but she couldn't bear that this...this wretch who had hurt and betrayed her sister should know it, too.

He was the one in the wrong, he was the one who had walked away, uncaring of the misery he left in his wake, not giving his broken-hearted victim a second thought. And the way he was looking at her, as if he knew she was telling a pack of lies, put her down on his contemptible level.

She couldn't bear that, either. It made her feel squirmy inside, nauseous, even, and she was on the point of beating a dignified retreat, forgetting the reason for her being here in the first place, when he unexpectedly and mildly defused the situation.

'Why don't you and Sophie get to know each other?' Gently but firmly, he put the little girl on her bare pink feet. Caroline huffed out her pent-up breath and relaxed her rigid shoulders. She had been on the point of walking out, her pride making her forget why she had come here, forfeiting her opportunity to somehow find a way to make him pay for what he had done.

DIANA HAMILTON   13

She would never, ever let him get to her like that again.

'Yes, why not?' she concurred, smiling at the child. That was easy. Clad in a miniature pair of white cotton dungarees and an apple-green T-shirt, the round-eyed moppet was adorable. Caroline's eyes flicked to the silver-framed photographs and back again to the baby.

Even at this tender age the resemblance was startling. The same fine, flaxen wavy hair—although of course the mother's was much, much longer—and the same piquant features and enormous dark brown eyes. Unusual colouring, bearing no resemblance whatsoever to her father. Caroline's smile widened as she saw dimples appear on either side of the rosebud mouth and then she sobered, wondering what the heck came next in the game of getting-to-know-you. Did fifteen-month-old babies walk? Did they talk? She had no idea!

Finn Helliar's eyes were on her, contemplative, knowing, almost as if he was fully aware of the way she was floundering, out of her depth. She looked away quickly, feeling her face go hot. Any minute now she would blow the whole thing.

Trouble was, she had never had anything whatsoever to do with young children. None of her friends were married and producing babies. Should she go and pick the moppet up? Would it scream if she did?

Thankfully, Sophie solved the problem. She launched herself from her father's steadying hands and toddled precariously across the few yards of carpet that separated them. Amber eyes widening with anxiety, Caroline leant forward and scooped the baby up before she could fall flat on her face. She plopped her down on her knees and, to counteract the feeling of being hot and bothered, said in what she hoped was a kindly yet authoritative nanny voice, 'Baby's walking very well for her age,' and hoped the pronouncement wasn't completely asinine.

No comment. A slight twitch of the mobile mouth. Caroline cuddled the baby defensively. The little body was warm and solid, a comforting shield against the clever, assessing eyes of the callous father.

'There is one thing—' Finn Helliar had unfolded his long, lean body from the armchair opposite the one she was using, walking with loping grace to lean against the sill of one of the tall windows. 'I would insist that Sophie's nanny wears mufti. Something pretty, feminine—' He gestured with one languid hand. 'I'm sure you get the picture. For a small child a starchy uniform could be off-putting.'

For a grown man, too, Caroline sniped to herself with a flash of cynicism. A man who could seduce someone as gullible as her sister Katie while getting another pregnant at the same time would want the females around him to look pretty.

And available?

That thought, coming out of nowhere, was repugnant. It was all she could do to keep quiet, to swallow what she wanted to say to him, to bide her time. And bide her time she must, if she were to find the very best way, the perfect way to force him to eat dirt and acknowledge the great, irreparable damage he had done.

*   *   *

'Well, you've done it now!' Mary Greaves said heavily.

Two years ago, Mary hadn't been wildly enthusiastic at accepting the then twenty-three-year-old Caro as a partner. But her nanny agency had been going downhill and she'd needed new capital, new ideas.

She'd fully expected her new young partner to be like her mother. She'd been at school with the mother but had lost touch until just recently. Emma Farr was a darling, sweet-natured and gentle, she recalled. But timid. A dreamer, not a doer.

But Caro, the elder of Emma's two girls, had proved to be just the opposite. Decisive, intelligent, a degree in business studies firmly in her pocket, she had turned the agency around, discarding the old name of Mommy's Helpers with the tilt of a finely arched brow, the stroke of a pen, re-naming it Grandes Familles and making it so, going straight for the wealthy, aristocratic French families because as far as they were concerned a British nanny was *de rigueur*.

And the partnership had worked; her own child-care experience, her ability to interview clients, discover exactly what they wanted, coupled with Caro's business brain, was proving a winner.

Now only dedicated, professional nannies were on their books, those with the very highest qualifications, and only those who could afford to pay to acquire the services of the very best approached the agency. It had all happened without her, Mary, having to do anything. Sometimes she felt positively over-awed by the much younger woman's sharpness of mind, her dedication to her work and breathtaking drive.

But now the high-flyer seemed to have flipped!

'Mr Helliar phoned through as soon as you left him. You're hired,' she stated even more heavily as she watched the lovely face before her turn white, then pink. 'For eight weeks. Starting tomorrow. He said, and I quote, ''Though eight minutes in my daughter's company would be enough to make anyone love her to bits, so she's on a loser there.'' I can't imagine what you've been saying to him—and for the sake of my blood pressure I'd rather not know.'

'Not a lot,' Caroline said truthfully, feeling behind her for her office chair and sinking down on it, feeling as if the stuffing had been knocked out of her.

There was much she could have said to the louse, none of it fit to be voiced in front of his delightful little daughter. So she should be congratulating herself for landing the job, thus giving herself the time she needed to discover the perfect way to pay him back for what he had done to Katie, instead of feeling suddenly way out of her depth.

'He asked for references but I thought I could stall him on that. Besides, I give you a week before you're begging me to find a replacement. By then you'll have had as much hands-on experience as you can take!' Mary said, perching on the edge of the desk, crossing her arms over her bolster-like bosom. 'I'll go through the files and find someone to step in and do a bit of damage limitation when you decide you've had enough.'

'I'm not a quitter; you know I'm not. And I won't do any damage.' Or only to his conscience.

She smiled warmly at her mother's old schoolfriend. Widowed young, childless, the agency was her *raison d'être*, and she wouldn't let her down. She was back firmly in control of herself again and knew she could handle the situation with Finn Helliar and emerge unscathed. The agency's reputation would be unmarred because the louse wouldn't dare say a word about having been landed with a nanny who knew nothing about the job, not after being made to understand exactly what a low-life he was.

She could understand Mary's alarm. Had the situation been reversed she would have strenuously vetoed the idea. 'Please don't worry,' she offered gently.

'Now why would I do that?' the older woman countered dryly. 'But seriously, though, you must understand that the position of a nanny is subservient. You are used to being the boss, or one of them, and for the next two months you will have to do as you are told, spend practically all of your time with a demanding child. I hope, for both our sakes, that you can handle it. And another thing; had I been able to place the nanny of my choice with Mr Helliar, I would have looked for someone far less young and beautiful—someone middle-aged and preferably plain.'

'Don't be silly!' Caroline pulled a sheet of paper towards her and began to make hurried notes of what she wanted Honor to attend to during her absence.

Mary grunted, 'Don't pretend to be stupid. Finn Helliar's a staggeringly attractive man. Living under the same roof, a beautiful young woman in a subservient position to—'

'I get the picture,' Caroline inserted tightly. She'd got more than that—the information that Mary had instinctively known that Helliar was the type of man who'd make a play for any presentable woman, the little matter of having a wife no deterrent at all.

*   *   *

Finn settled Sophie down for her afternoon nap, his gaze lingering lovingly on her cherubic face, the huge brown eyes closed in sleep. 'A nanny to play with tomorrow, my pet,' he whispered softly, more to himself than to the child. 'Won't that be fun?'

He walked quietly from the room, leaving the door ajar so he could hear her when she woke. And fun it would be—intriguing to find out exactly why Caroline Farr had decided to work as a nanny, out of her own agency.

At one point he had considered asking her, had fully intended to. But after she'd given him that spiel about knitting and fairy cakes he'd known he wouldn't get a straight answer.

It had quickly become obvious that she was unaware that he knew who she was—the go-getting half of the Grandes Familles partnership.

Her grandmother, Elinor Farr, had never tired of boasting of her favourite grandchild's intelligence, determination and spirit. She had even, on one of the rare occasions when he'd visited Farr Place—that almost laughably Gothic pile in one of the most secluded parts of Hertfordshire—brought out the family photograph album and pointed out the woman he was already beginning to regard as a pain in the neck.

'Caroline's the only one left fit to carry the Farr name,' the formidable old matriarch had stated. 'Her mother's a simpering fool and as for her sister—well, Katie wouldn't say boo to a fly—let alone a goose!'

Dragooned into staying on for the old lady's eightieth birthday party, with which his visit had unfortunately coincided, he had felt sorry for the inhabitants of the lodge—Elinor's browbeaten daughter-in-law and younger grandchild, Katie. It must be galling to be watched over with such fierce contempt by the old lady who held the purse-strings so tightly in her bony, heavily be-ringed hands, to be compared so unfavourably with the do-no-wrong Caroline. He had been glad that a dose of flu had prevented her turning up.

Sorry, in another kind of way, for Elinor herself. The daughter of a general, she had joined her considerable private fortune to that of Ambrose Farr on their marriage. A marriage which had produced only one child. She must have been devastated when her son was killed on the hunting field when Caroline was a mere five years old, the baby, Katie, not quite one.

The death of Ambrose, her husband, a few months later would have been another shattering blow. But she had recovered, ruled what remained of her family with a rod of iron and, with the advice of his father, then chairman of the family-owned merchant bank, had tied everything up in trust funds.

Since his father's death he had taken his place as Elinor Farr's financial advisor, for the sake of the link of friendship between his father and the deceased Ambrose. Not, on the whole, an onerous task, his contact with the old lady being rare, his personal visits rarer.

His London office had dealt with the transfer of monies from one of the funds to provide the capital to buy Caroline Farr into partnership, and the last time he'd spoken to Elinor she'd been full of how well the agency was doing now that Caroline was running the business side of things.

But was it doing well? Or was the agency in trouble? Why else should one of the partners, sketchily trained, or, more likely, not trained at all, leave her executive persona behind, put on a stiff and starchy nanny uniform and sally forth to change other people's babies' nappies if the outfit wasn't desperately in need of the extra funds?

He picked up a pile of glossy estate agents' brochures and grinned. One way or another, he'd find out why she'd been driven to look for temporary, extra-curricular employment. And it would be no hardship, no hardship at all. Even in that smothering grey suit and awful hat she'd been lovely to look at, and he'd glimpsed an impish sense of humour when she'd listed her so-called hobbies.

He could live with that. For a few weeks. He'd given himself three months' leave to settle permanently back in England, find the sort of home where Sophie could spend a happy childhood, so he'd be on hand at all times to oversee closely the new nanny's doings.

And there was no danger he'd find himself in the same tricky situation he'd been plunged into with her sister, Katie.

Caroline was different. Older by five years, a mature woman, sophisticated, street-wise. She wouldn't give him any trouble.

Not that kind of trouble.

CHAPTER TWO

CAROLINE hadn't been in her new employment for more than five minutes before she was seething. Absolutely seething! The beastly man was at it again!

Quickly, Caroline scooped the baby up into her arms and held her close and felt the little face press into her neck, blowing bubbles. She cradled the back of the golden head with a gentle hand, keeping it safely where it was, regardless of tickling bubbles, blown raspberries and baby-type giggles. She would do anything to prevent the innocent little scrap from seeing her father coming on to a woman who was not her mother!

When she'd arrived at ten that morning Finn had shown her to her quarters, a suite within a suite. A large sunny bedroom holding all the usual furniture, plus a cot complete with teddy bear. *En suite* bathroom, nicely luxurious, with a baby bath on a stand. Plus a small sitting room, the carpet lavishly littered with toys, comfortable armchairs, TV and writing desk. And Sophie, clad only in a disposable nappy, crawling around the furniture as if going for some kind of land-speed record.

'I'll leave you to settle in.' He'd smiled, his eyes warm with discomfiting male appreciation as they'd languorously swept her slender figure. 'Like the dress. Pretty. It suits you far better than that dark thing you were wearing yesterday.'

21

Oh, did it? It was floral cotton, years old, did he but know it. She hadn't dressed to please him, or only inasmuch as he'd stipulated mufti, so he needn't think it! Amber scorn had glinted at him between tangled dark lashes but had been rapidly veiled as she'd caught the devilish silver mockery of his eyes.

Her breath had tugged, stuck in her chest and hurt, but he'd turned away, saying to his daughter, 'Come and say hello to Caro, poppet. It's time you were dressed.' And he'd then said, obviously to her—although she hadn't looked at him, kept her eyes glued to the bottoms of his lightweight fawn trousers where they touched the top of his bare feet. Bare feet?—'Do say if it goes against all your training, but I thought Caro more infant-friendly than the formal title of Nanny. And Caroline's a bit of a mouthful.' And, when she'd failed to answer because she was too busy wondering about the odd inflexion when he'd mentioned 'all your training', he'd imparted lightly, 'She'll probably need her nappy changing, but leave it. I'll be back in a couple of minutes and you can let me in on your theories on toilet training later.'

Caroline had gulped. She knew of no theories. She'd have to make them up as she went along. But at least he'd left, walking out of the room into the main living area, although leaving the door to her quarters wide open, she noted now suspiciously.

As if he intended to watch her, check up on what she was doing, even though he'd told her he'd be back in no time.

It simply wasn't on. Having him watch her fumbling attempts to dress his child was a bad idea.

Having him watch her, in any capacity, was a worse one. The very thought of it made her feel overheated.

She walked to the door to close it, the soft skirts of her dress brushing against the long, silky lines of her legs. And stopped in the open doorway, appalled.

Finn had admitted a woman into the main suite. A very polished, beautiful woman. Not his wife. This one had short dark hair, cut in a modern, sophisticated style. Very sharp. Pale skin, scarlet lips, dark blue silk dress with a bloused top and cleavage. And what a cleavage!

The moment he'd pushed the door to behind his guest, Finn slipped an arm around the slender waist, pulling her to him, then bent to drop a kiss on the invitingly upturned, poutily scarlet lips.

It couldn't have been much of a kiss because none of the red had come off on his mouth, Caro noted, brows beetling as they walked further into the body of the room as if permanently joined at the hip. But even so...

She decided to use her authority as nanny to tell him, at a suitable moment, of course, that she wouldn't permit such carryings-on in front of her charge. She wouldn't mention Fleur—naturally she wouldn't; their marriage wasn't any of her business. But she could justly claim that the baby was.

Seeing her in the open doorway, the baby held protectively in her arms, Finn grinned broadly. 'The two of you make a pretty picture. Nice.' Which probably accounted for the way the newcomer raised perfectly arched brows above the suddenly icy blue eyes that swept dismissively over the softly faded cotton dress to drift up again to meet amber scorn with a chilling sneer.

'So you found a suitable minder.' The woman was obviously bored, but sounded far more interested in her next pronouncement. 'With Mrs Helliar being away you've been so tied down. You can get yourself a life now. Have fun.'

'This is Sandra,' Finn introduced. 'My personal secretary from the London office.' Perhaps something about the unconcealed disapproval in Caroline's eyes got through to him because he moved sideways, putting a distance of an inch or two between him and the curvy, silk-clad body as he dropped his arm from her waist. 'I've taken a few weeks' leave to go house-hunting, get settled back in England, but I still like to know what's going on. Sandra keeps me posted.'

And Sandra had moved back in, close to his big body, joining them at the hip again. Sandra was not willing to be deprived of what she wanted, Caroline noted, her hackles rising when the other woman smiled winningly up into her employer's face and cooed, 'Did you get the particulars from the estate agents? I emphasised you needed them at once.' And, not waiting for an answer, she added, 'Perhaps thingy—the nanny—could make coffee. We could go through the particulars while we drink it.'

'That is a job for a secretary, not the nanny,' 'thingy' responded tartly, and closed the door on the pair of them, muttering.

He certainly believed in spreading himself around! He didn't go for a particular type, either. Secretary Sandra could look out for herself, no problem. She would be only too willing to play games in the absence of his wife, and wouldn't be too demanding, or make a nuisance of herself. A fat bonus in her pay packet would suffice, and she'd be happy to put in a bit of discreet 'overtime' when his wife returned.

Katie had been different. Katie had completely broken down after Finn Helliar had seduced her, promised her the earth, then promptly married another woman, the one who was expecting his child.

And he hadn't married Fleur because he loved her; he wouldn't have seduced Katie if he had. The brute was obviously incapable of committing himself to one woman. But he'd been caught in the age-old trap and he was clearly not averse to having a child. Much as she disliked admitting it, so far she couldn't fault the way he was with his baby daughter.

The pregnancy wouldn't have been deliberate, but Finn had been relaxed enough about the prospect of fatherhood to marry the mother and drop poor bewitched Katie flat. Plus half a dozen others, in all probability.

Was that why Fleur was conspicuous by her absence? Had she discovered, after marriage, that her husband was constitutionally unfitted for monogamy? Was that why she was, presumably, re-launching her career?

She set the now squirming baby down on her feet. 'Come on, poppet, time to get dressed.' She looked down into the happy little face and felt a great pang of protectiveness engulf her. It was a similar feeling to the one she had whenever her gran had a go at her mum and Katie.

Poor little scrap. With a father like Finn Helliar she was to be pitied, because unless her mother was remarkably forbearing she'd end up as yet another broken home statistic.

'Room Service will be delivering lunch in five minutes,' Finn said. Caroline glared at him, bristling with dislike. He had got rid of Sandra in next to no time, invaded the nanny suite, hovering over her while she'd bathed and dressed his daughter, just as if he didn't trust her to do anything properly. He was still hovering and, right at this moment, his child was investigating her new nanny's luggage and trying to strangle herself with one of Caro's bras—the one with pink rosebuds and lacy bits.

'Five minutes,' he reiterated, unwinding the bra from his daughter's chubby hands and neck, scooping her into the crook of his arm, his obvious but silent amusement alarming as he eyed the scrap of lacy material for a few tense fizzing moments then swept his gaze over her now fluttering bosom for even longer.

This time he closed the door behind him and that gave her a little breathing space, but nowhere near enough.

The dreadful man was getting to her, no doubt about it. The way he'd looked at her had been an insult, making her flesh tingle, and her heart was pounding so hard she thought it would choke her.

His sex appeal was awe-inspiring. And he knew it.

She brushed her hair, transforming the baby-rumpled mess into its usual glossy bob, deliberately not allowing her eyes to wander lower than her neck or higher than her chin. The caressing, lingering stroke of those come-to-bed eyes had done alarming things to her physiognomy.

The first, unguarded glance in the mirror had given her an image of glittering golden eyes and lips that looked softer, fuller than usual, parted in mindless anticipation.

Anticipation, pray, of what? she demanded of herself, hating the way her breasts were pushing at the soft cotton of her dress, refusing to let her eyes wander and witness that piece of humiliation.

If his technique was good enough to make level-headed, no one-tangles-with-me Caroline Farr respond to it, albeit unwillingly, what chance had poor Katie had?

No chance at all.

This observation thankfully counteracted the effect of those seemingly endless moments of sizzling sexual appraisal and sent her into the bathroom to run cold water over her wrists. It also enabled her to march sturdily out into the main living area to endure the horror of having to share a meal with him. But the experience wasn't as distasteful as she'd expected it to be—not to begin with.

For one thing his attention was entirely on his daughter, on the small tasks of fastening her into the high chair, tying her bib, serving her with vegetables, pouring cheese sauce over the small helping of cauliflower and mashing it all together with the back of his fork.

Caro, feeling redundant, said, 'I'll take Sophie for a walk in the park this afternoon.' It would get her out of here for an hour or two. She was beginning to feel decidedly trapped.

'Sophie has a nap in the afternoons.'

Was there condemnation in the tone, as if he was

telling her, in a roundabout way, that she didn't know anything? Well, he'd be right.

To cover herself, she remarked repressively, 'Naturally she does, Mr Helliar. I merely decided she would benefit from taking that nap while out in the fresh air of the park.' She had noted a folding pushchair in the small entrance lobby of the suite and that was what nannies did, wasn't it—push their charges endlessly round in the fresh air?

She felt, watching him gently wrap Sophie's small fingers round the full plastic teaspoon, that she had put herself in a position of control. She had 'decided', had neatly sidestepped his suspicions about her ability—had he had any—and put herself firmly in charge.

Until he said, 'Fine; we'll go together.'

Her stomach lurched. She put the forkful of grilled Dover sole back down on her plate. She had suggested the outing to escape his company, not get more of it!

She needed the time and space; heaven knew she did. So far she had not had a single moment to herself to even begin to work out how to pay him back for what he had done to Katie.

'That won't be necessary, Mr Helliar.' Said sweetly and, she thought, reasonably, but he glanced across the table at her, his silver eyes probing, and not probing gently, either.

'The name's Finn. And I decide what's necessary.'

That figured. She regrouped and began another attack, cloaked in common sense.

'You employed me to look after Baby, Mr—Finn. Presumably to free you up to do other things.' Hadn't the sultry Sandra gloated that at last he could get himself a life? Caro was frankly surprised he wasn't doing just that right now, given his track record. 'If you question my ability to look after my charge more than adequately...'

She left the implication hanging in the air, marvelling at her own temerity. He had been standing over her while she'd been dressing Sophie so he had to have noticed the way she'd put the baby's nappy on. She'd pulled the sticky tape thing too far on one side, leaving the other side barely connected, and the whole bunchy, lopsided bundle was held in place only by the intelligent choice of minute emerald-green shorts for nether-region wear. So he'd know that 'adequate' didn't get a look in when applied to her non-existent child-care abilities.

He didn't look up from his meal, which he was enjoying with the air of a man completely at ease with himself. Just told her, 'No one's questioning anything. I fancy some fresh air and exercise, in the company of my daughter. OK?'

It would have to be, since she wasn't in a position to forbid him to do anything. She lifted her fork again and began to wonder if by believing she could force him to acknowledge what he'd done to Katie she was making a complete fool of herself. She was sure of it when he added, replying to her earlier statement, 'I employed a nanny—you, as it happens—so that Sophie could get used to having someone else look after her while I'm still around, before I start nine-to-five-ing again.'

Not one mention of when his wife might return to take his place. Which didn't augur well for the innocent poppet. Was her mother so disillusioned with her marriage that she intended to devote herself full-time to re-launching her career, making flying visits to her little daughter when and if she could spare the time?

She wasn't going to ask, wasn't going to involve herself in their domestic troubles, because she had enough on her mind without adding to her burdens, and she put the blame for everything firmly at Finn's feet.

They ended up in the Rose Garden, the beautiful blooms making the warm July afternoon heavy with perfume. Finn noted the rapt expression on Caro's face. She had lost that prim and starchy look and it was a revelation. She was beautiful.

The snapshots Elinor Farr had paraded for his inspection had depicted serious, symmetrical features and wide, impatient eyes. He had barely glanced at them, already dismissing the absent, favourite grandchild as a prig, too good to be true, tired of hearing how all-fired wonderful she was in comparison with her mother and sister, both of whom he had felt immediately and instinctively sorry for.

But reality, as she bent to cup a bloom and inhale its heady fragrance, was a softly sensual smile and a gentle curve of glossy hair the colour of burnished chestnuts which fell forward to caress creamy, apricot-tinted skin and reveal the elegant, delicate length and slenderness of her neck above the graceful curve of a body at once fragile yet utterly, gloriously feminine.

Something jerked inside his chest. He wanted to ask her what was wrong, if her business was going downhill, if she was in danger of losing her capital. To tell her right now that he knew who she was and she could trust him. He wanted to help.

He wanted, quite suddenly, to touch, to take her delicate hands in his, to end the subterfuge and offer his considerable financial expertise, quite freely. If she was in some kind of a mess then he could help her get out of it.

But for some reason he couldn't formulate the words. There was a tightness in the muscles of his throat, a strange constriction. And then it all became academic because Sophie was waking, babbling baby talk and wriggling in her pushchair, wanting out.

So they would go to the boating lake to look at the ducks, and tonight, over dinner, when his daughter was tucked up and asleep, he'd speak to Caro, discover the truth, he promised himself.

It was important that there should be no equivocation between them. Just how important he was yet to realise.

CHAPTER THREE

'JUST one more spoonful, there's a good girl!' Caro
registered the pleading whine in her voice and was
horrified. Where had her Nanny-knows-best-and-
won't-be-thwarted voice disappeared to? But Finn had
opted for a quick shower and she'd so wanted to give
the baby her supper and prove to him that she could
do something right.

'Lovely onion soup!' she cried more bracingly, remembering how she had doted on the stuff as a child.
But she must have had depraved taste buds, she decided glumly as Sophie blew a monster raspberry and
showered her with the despised offering.

'Having trouble?' Finn, tucking the tails of a crisp
white shirt into the waistband of narrow-fitting slate-
grey trousers, walked into the sitting room of her
suite, eyeing the cross red face of his infant daughter.

Sophie's mouth went square as soon as she saw her
father, and Finn plucked her out of the high chair to
take her mind off onion soup and nip the wailing session in the bud. 'She usually has a boiled egg followed by fruit for her supper.' He looked unbearably
smug, as if he'd given her a test, knowing she'd fail,
and felt superior because he'd proved himself right.

Caro wanted to hit him for walking in and discovering her ineptness—for walking in at all when she'd
imagined she'd seen the last of him for the evening
after their return from the park—quality time, he'd

called it. Before disappearing he'd told her, 'Sophie
has supper around now. Ring Room Service. You'll
find the kitchen staff very accommodating.'

At a huge disadvantage, covered in onion soup as
she was, Caro tried to salvage something and managed to find some dignity as she told him, 'Onions
cleanse the blood.' Everyone knew that, didn't they?
And she watched him tuck the baby more securely
into the crook of his arm as he went to the phone in
the main living room, and wondered whether the snort
he gave denoted scorn or amusement at her expense.

Deciding she didn't give a damn either way, she
began to tidy away the mess Sophie had made, making herself stay calm because in the not too distant
future he would be the one who was cringing.

He'd showered and changed so he'd be going out
for the evening, which was lovely. She'd bath the
baby and put her to bed and spend her own evening
plotting the best way to hurt his conscience.

But she immediately felt mortified when the waiter
carried through the revised supper on a tray. A boiled
egg in a cup decorated with rabbits wearing blue bon-
nets, a similarly decorated bowl of diced fresh fruit
and a plate of thinly sliced bread and butter.

It was worse still when Finn followed through with
Sophie. She was wearing a fresh bib and her sunniest
smile and Caro, feeling ridiculous, just standing there
clutching the toast soldiers she'd gathered up from the
floor where the baby had flung them, realised that
Mary had been right when she'd said she was crazy.

She should never have got herself in so deep. More
at home with balance sheets, with interviewing nannies who were anxious to be adopted by the now pres-

tigious Grandes Familles Agency or wealthy parents from the UK and America, as well as France, who wanted only the very best for their offspring, than dealing with offspring, she felt like an idiot.

For the first time in her life she felt like giving up on a project. She could contact Mary and ask her to send that replacement, the one who was probably already on the starting-block. And bow out.

She couldn't alter the way he was. Nothing she could say to him, no matter how stinging, would make a scrap of difference. He would go on using women all through his life, never giving them a second thought once he had tired of them, never looking back or wondering what had happened to them. How could she hurt his conscience if he didn't have one?

'Why don't you go and freshen up? I can feed this little monster,' Finn suggested lightly, smiling to show he wasn't about to put on his outraged employer's hat.

She looked vulnerable, beaten, her soft mouth drooping, the eyes that had swept momentarily to his as he'd spoken spangled with tears. He found he couldn't bear that. He hated it. Deeply.

Something was wrong and he wanted to help put it right and he couldn't do that unless she opened up and talked to him, told him what the problem was. Whatever her grandmother's opinion, she wasn't Wonderwoman. His shoulders were broad enough to carry the burden that was so clearly dragging her down. And with a woman as lovely as Caroline Farr that would be no problem. In fact, he decided suddenly, it would be a pleasure.

With Sophie secured in her high chair and munch-

ing on bread and butter he moved quickly to the for-
lorn yet graceful figure in her soup-spattered cotton
dress. She was no more a nanny than he was, knew
much less about child care—and he was no expert.
He just muddled along as best he could, taking his
daughter's happiness as the yardstick and to hell with
timetables and theories.

'Give yourself a break.' The gruffness of his voice
surprised him. So far she hadn't moved. This close,
he could smell the fresh floral fragrance of her—the
perfume she used, he supposed. Or was it the essence
of the woman herself?

He cleared his throat. 'Give me that.' He meant the
discarded pieces of toast she held in her hands. His
fingers brushed the slender length of hers and something happened. Something wild and sweet and un-
restrained.

She felt it, too. He saw the shaft of surprise in the
golden gleam between tangled dark lashes and heard
the harsh sound of her swiftly sucking in her breath.
And then her chin came up, her head turning sharply
on the graceful line of her neck and shoulders, small
hands decisive as they snatched away from his.

Unrestraint was ruled out of play. Which was probably just as well, he thought, watching the sway of
her hips as she went to dispose of the mangled toast
in the waste bin. He needed to uncover the truth, find
out why she was here, doing a job she was patently
untrained for, before—

Before? That implied that something would come
after. And that, surely, was nonsense.

Or was it?

*   *   *

Caro closed the bathroom door behind her and leaned against it, mourning the lack of a lock. She needed a shower. She felt hot and bothered, sticky all over.

The thought of him walking in on her was terrifying. He was potent stuff and if she'd learned anything in the few hours she'd been here it was that she was no more immune to him than the rest of womankind.

She remembered the way she'd felt when he'd touched her hands, standing so close she would have melted into him had she swayed on her feet by the smallest fraction. The brush of his skin against hers had made her want to do just that, as if something deep inside her was answering a call as old as time.

But—and it was a very big but—she knew exactly what an unprincipled womaniser he was. She wasn't about to walk into the jaws of a smiling tiger. She might be as crazy as Mary had said, but she wasn't that crazy!

And he wouldn't walk in on her while she was in the shower, she rationalised. It would be classified as sexual harassment and she could get him blacklisted by all the agencies around.

Heartened by the resurgence of her fighting spirit, she stripped off and turned on the shower head. It wasn't like her to throw in the towel.

When she recalled how her eyes had filled with stupid tears because of the kindness of his smile, the gentle warmth of the suggestion that she go and freshen up while he saw to Sophie, along with her own unusual and abhorrent feelings of ineptitude, she could scarcely believe she was capable of such weakness. How could she have been such a wimp?

No, the plan was still on, all systems go. She'd

muddle through as best she could until she decided what form her retribution would take, or her name wasn't Caroline Farr!

Twenty minutes later, dressed now in a white T-shirt and black cotton trousers, her hair freshly blow-dried, she walked out of the bathroom, feeling brisk.

He could accuse her of not knowing much but he couldn't prove she wasn't a bona fide nanny.

She found Finn in the main sitting room, sprawled out on one of the sofas watching the news on TV, his mother-naked baby sitting right beside him, all big brown eyes, bouncy curls and seraphic smile.

'We used my bathroom for her ablutions.' His drawl was laid-back, lazy. 'It's bedtime, but we didn't want to invade your privacy.'

She supposed she should be a good little hireling and thank him nicely for his thoughtfulness. But didn't. And couldn't help noting the way he and his daughter were always a definite 'we', as if the baby had as much say in what went on as he did.

Before that could soften the way she regarded him, she responded coolly, 'Very well, Mr Helliar. I'll get her ready.' She scooped the baby up and hoped to heaven the child wouldn't volubly object because she wouldn't know what to do if she did.

Panic subsided as a chubby pair of arms went around her neck, the baby's head snuggling comfortably beneath her chin. Caro walked to the set of rooms she shared with Sophie, her back straight and her head held high with the pride of achievement, as if she'd worked a minor miracle, no problem.

Further miracles became manifest. One, she managed to put the nappy on properly. Two, she also slid the seemingly boneless little body snugly into the cotton sleeper she'd found stashed in one of the drawers without any hassle worth the name. And three, the baby's eyes were already drooping as she laid her in her cot.

Such was the power of positive thinking, she told herself. Then peace blew up in her face as Finn murmured from behind her, 'Shall I sing her to sleep, or would you rather do it?'

Her breath froze in her lungs with shock. Why did he have to creep up on her like that, making her jump out of her skin? He seemed to find it impossible to leave her alone with his daughter for more than a few minutes at a time. Tension bunched up her shoulder muscles until they hurt. And why did he have to stand so close?

'She'll want her daddy.' She had her voice back, but only just. 'I'm still a virtual stranger.' She walked out of the room then, quickly, softly, and stood in front of the now blank TV screen, staring at it, wondering how Fleur could leave her gorgeous little daughter for as much as a minute.

'She went out like a light.'

He was doing it again, creeping up behind her, his voice too darn soft, too warm and honeyed.

'Good.' What else could she say? She moved a few paces away from him and her heartbeats slowed a little. Then everything inside her dropped—heart, lungs, lights and liver—right down to the soles of her feet; it was a miracle that she stayed upright at all, she marvelled as she wallowed in the agitated aftermath of his simple words:

'We'll eat dinner here. Room Service will deliver any time now.'

'You're going out,' she managed at last. She wanted him out. She needed time on her own to plot and scheme, didn't she? She couldn't think straight when he was around. He muddled her and she was totally unused to being muddled. She couldn't bear it!

'News to me.' He flipped through the television listings then tossed the magazine back on a low coffee table. He didn't look like a man who would contentedly spend a night in flicking through the channels to find something he wanted to watch then going to bed early with a good book when he couldn't.

From what she'd heard of him he would want to be out and about, seeing friends. Female friends. Hadn't Sandra opined that he could now get himself a life? And the way she'd looked at him when she'd said it meant she would willingly be in on the action.

So why wasn't he taking the opportunity? Because he wasn't as black as her second-hand knowledge had painted him or because—and this seemed far more likely—he didn't want to leave her alone with his baby daughter?

That was logical. She was comfortable with logic. For all he was a callous, heartless brute where women were concerned, no one could deny he adored his child. And the new nanny had been here for less than twenty-four hours and had shown herself to be largely incompetent.

She gave him a good attempt at a reassuring smile and said calmly, 'Sophie will be fine with me, if that's what's troubling you. I'm perfectly capable of attending to her should she wake. Didn't your *secretary*—'

she invested that word with heavy emphasis, quite deliberately '—say you could now get yourself a life? So why don't you? I'm sure she'd be more than happy to help you get back in the swing of things.'

Gross impertinence, given her subordinate position; she knew that and didn't give a fig. She wanted to draw him out, hear him add to the list of his sins with his own far too sexy mouth.

And he did. In a way he did. He said, looking at her with enigmatic silver eyes, 'Oh, yes, I'm quite sure she would. But not tonight.'

Tonight he had plans. Tonight he meant to delve and dig and discover why she was here. He found he had a sudden urgency to get to know her a great deal better, find out what made this woman tick. This oddly prickly, supremely lovely, breath-catchingly graceful woman.

Then, as a discreet tap on the door heralded the arrival of the room-service waiter with his trolley, he added, 'Neither am I troubled. Once she's asleep Sophie never wakes. But as we're going to be practically living in each other's pockets for the next few months I thought we should spend an hour or so getting to know each other better. Hitting the town can wait.'

Caro, watching the waiter set out the covers on the table in the window, felt her stomach lurch, twist and contract. He meant to quiz her about her credentials; a little late in the day of course, but doubtless brought on by her obvious and total lack of experience.

She'd fudge her way through that somehow; she could have done without it but the prospect didn't bother her too much. What was really churning her

up was the way he'd as good as admitted he had
something going with that secretary of his.

'Not tonight', he'd said, implying that there were
plenty of other nights when he'd take the opportunity
to play away from home. What kind of normal married man would have made such an admission to the
newly hired nanny?

But he wasn't a normal married man. He'd made
his wedding vows but he didn't mean to keep them.
The type of man who could treat Katie the way he
had was capable of anything.

'Shall we eat?' His warm, dark voice made her
spine prickle in none too subtle warning. Inadvertently, she glanced up and met his eyes. If his mouth
was sexy, his eyes were more so. They pulled her into
the softly gleaming silver depths with an invitation
that was hard to resist.

'I'm not really hungry.' She found her voice; it was
strangely husky. That intimate, come-to-bed look was
carefully cultivated, part of his stock-in-trade, guar-
anteed to set female hearts fluttering.

But not this female's heart. Sweet, naive Katie with
her fragile self-esteem had been a pushover. Two
years ago, at barely eighteen, her little sister had met
this man and been blown away like a leaf in a hur-
ricane, had believed every rotten lie he'd told her and
suffered the shattering consequences.

'It's the heat,' he sympathised. 'But you must try
to eat something.'

His words penetrated the dark fog of her rage,
pushed her into getting a grip on herself.

'I'll do my best.' Her voice was empty, her movements brisk and businesslike as she walked to the table, seated herself and glanced at what was on offer.

Cold poached salmon, slices of chicken breast in a lemon sauce, a multiplicity of salads. She barely listened to his idle comments about the heatwave, the noise and air pollution of the never-sleeping capital, the undesirability of bringing up a child in a city. She kept her eyes on her plate or on the tree-lined street beyond the window, the dusty leaves at eye-level.

Only when he put in, 'How's the agency doing? From what I was told, Grandes Familles was an overnight success,' did she allow herself to look at him.

There was a subtle challenge there somewhere. He didn't strike her as the type of man who would be interested in idle gossip and she knew that his father had helped her gran set up those convoluted trust funds after her grandpa had died.

Would he be aware that capital from one of the funds had been used by the agency? Hardly likely. Such small beer would be beneath the notice of the powerful chief executive; the release would have been dealt with at a much lower level.

And he wouldn't connect her surname with the name of the barely ex-schoolgirl he had seduced and abandoned two years ago. Farr was a fairly common name. He probably couldn't remember Katie's name in any case.

In any case, had he leaped to the conclusion that because her surname was Farr she had to be connected to Katie, then surely he would have mentioned it by now? She was, she assured herself staunchly, getting away with it!

So it was just idle conversation and her cover

wasn't blown. She picked up her as yet untouched glass of wine and twirled it slowly round by the stem.

'How should I know? It gets a good press. I only signed on with them recently.' It was a blessing she wasn't Pinocchio or by now her nose would have reached right over the table, probably poking holes in the crisp white shirt that covered those mightily impressive shoulders.

'I see. How long have you been working as a nanny?' Finn leant back in his chair, watching the film of colour rise beneath her skin. He didn't need that, or the way she suddenly buried her nose in her wine glass, to tell him she was hiding something. Telling lies to cover the truth.

Which was? His narrowed eyes lingered on the attenuated line of her throat as she tipped her glass, drinking deeply. That she had no idea he knew who she was and had already guessed she'd turned her hand to nannying to bring in desperately needed extra funds.

She and her partner, the pleasant, capable-seeming middle-aged woman who'd interviewed him initially, wouldn't want it known that their high-flying agency had taken a nose-dive.

'Not long.' She answered his question when her glass was empty and she could no longer find an excuse to keep silent. But at least it was the truth. Less than twenty-four hours, in fact. A sudden urge to giggle had her wondering if swallowing that wine had been one of the best ideas she'd ever had.

So she wasn't going to come clean. He could wait. Finn refilled her glass from the bottle of Moselle he'd ordered. She barely knew him, after all. She would hardly take him into her confidence so soon, and he was reluctant to force it out of her by telling her he knew she was the other half—the driving half—of the partnership.

He wanted her to trust him enough to share her problems with him, and so allow him to help her get to grips with them. He wanted those problems, and the subterfuge, out of the way. And he knew the perfect way to hasten that happy event. He had already made up his mind. To gain her trust he needed a more intimate atmosphere than an impersonal hotel suite could provide.

'I'd like you to pack for you and Sophie first thing in the morning.' Her attention was back on him again, her eyes wide and golden, completely without artifice, mildly questioning. Beautiful. He held them, his voice soft as he told her, 'We're moving to the country. A cottage just big enough for the three of us. Secluded, peaceful, a good place to draw breath.' His eyes were drawn without his say-so to her mouth. A soft mouth, the colour of crushed strawberries and probably just as sweet.

Or sweeter. And open now. The parted, berry-sweet lips held him fascinated as he said in a voice he barely recognised as his own, 'You'd like that?'

CHAPTER FOUR

'NOT a lot!' The words were snapped out before Caro could stop them.

A secluded country cottage, just the three of them—and a fifteen-month-old toddler hardly counted as a chaperon—sounded definitely something to avoid, given his despicable womanising inclinations.

It wasn't what he had actually said but the way he had said it that had set alarm bells ringing. But to keep the nanny pretence up and running she should have acceded to whatever her employer had suggested with a calm 'Of course, whatever you say, sir'.

Too late now, though. She presented him with a face as blank as she could possibly make it while she waited to discover what he'd make of this further insubordination and noted that, impossibly, he appeared to be smothering laughter.

'So you're a city girl.' He noticed her taut features. In all probability that was a natural reaction to a childhood spent in rural Hertfordshire, physically isolated by the vastness of the family estate, mentally dominated by that scratchy old matriarch, Elinor Farr. It made sense, and at least she'd been up front about that. It was a start.

'Come with me.' He left the table and her eyes raked suspiciously over the lean length of him. He looked great. Nature had given him the perfect male physique, added a few barrowloads of laid-back charm and topped off the recipe with more simmering sex appeal than was good for him or womankind.

Swallowing some sort of obstruction that was annoyingly clogging her throat, Caro reluctantly followed him to the sofa and sank down on the empty space beside him which he was patting invitingly.

Evening sunlight was streaming through the windows, touching his skin with gold, glancing off the coppery highlights in his thick dark hair. Caro swallowed another lump and forced her eyes away, fastening them on the sheaf of estate agents particulars he was extracting from a glossy folder.

She didn't want to find anything about him appealing; it would be a type of betrayal, both to herself and her darling little sister. She would remind herself of that every time she found herself watching him, inadvertently admiring the way he looked.

'I'm house-hunting, as you know, and I've got the details of three properties in Bedfordshire here, any one of which could fit the bill, but obviously I need to view.' Long, blunt-ended fingers flicked through the glossy pages. 'A friend of mine has a weekend cottage in the area as it happens. He offered me the use of it while he and his family are holidaying abroad, and I think we could find ways to make good use of it, don't you?'

He leaned back, angling wide, hard shoulders into the corner of the sofa, his eyes holding hers with an intimacy that was shocking, his smile pure wickedness as he drawled softly, 'The idea must appeal, surely?'

Not in the least. In fact it gave her the shivers because Finn Helliar was surely flirting with her; what he had said about finding ways of making good use of a secluded country cottage had been loaded with suggestions she didn't want to even contemplate.

Wisely, though, she held her tongue, and was glad she had when he elaborated, apparently quite harmlessly, 'It will make a handy base for viewing all three properties and it will do us all good to get some fresh clean air into our lungs. And I can't wait to see what Sophie makes of fields with cows in them and trees with apples growing on them instead of coming in paper bags from the greengrocer's.'

Waxing lyrical now, was he? Caro gave him a withering look, excused herself, and went to bed.

Caro woke to a room filled with summer morning sunshine, baby-babble, and the insistent rattling of the bars of the cot.

'Hi there, poppet!' Caro rolled off the mattress, tugged down the hem of the worn old T-shirt she wore to bed and lifted the small bundle of vivacious energy out from the cot. And spent the next hour playing with her charge.

Sophie, she discovered, could say lots of comprehensible words, most of them loudly. The loudest of which was 'Horn!', which became positively stentorian until they'd up-ended the toy box and found, right at the bottom, a squashy, lop-eared blue velvet rabbit.

'Horn!' Sophie bellowed happily, clutching the floppy rabbit to her tiny chest, her huge brown eyes bright with mischief.

Caro sat back on her heels, making herself nearer to child-height. 'Time to get dressed. And I guess you should have a bath. Am I right?'

'No, no, no, naughty!' The bright head shook vigorously, setting blonde curls bouncing. 'Bears. Do bears!'

Caro gave up as the toddler squirmed out of her gentle grasp and set off through the suite on all fours, dragging Horn behind her.

The nanny bit would have to wait and Sophie's giggles and squeals were infectious. Caro gave pursuit on her hands and knees, making growly noises, making the squeals and giggles coming from her charge ever louder; she couldn't remember when she'd had this much fun!

'Do you have to make quite so much noise?' The dark voice, coming from right behind her, was like a bucketful of ice-cold water.

Caro scrambled to her feet, tugging the soft fabric of the T-shirt as far down her thighs as it would go, conscious of his deep irritation and the wild sight she had to present, face red from doing growly noises, her body barely decently covered...

'Sophie should be dressed by now,' he grated, his dark brows lowered as he watched his daughter crawl under the cot at the speed of light, chortling merrily. 'Breakfast will arrive in five minutes. Have you packed? I said we'd be making an early start, remember?'

Caroline Farr felt inexpressibly silly. It swamped her, making her skin burn with embarrassed humiliation. Where was the cool businesswoman now, the one who had been coldly intent on revenge?

And where was the laid-back charmer? Not a sign of him in this mean and moody-looking male, clad in an ensemble of long-sleeved black cotton shirt and hip-hugging dark jeans that made him look definitely dangerous.

She took a tentative step towards the cot but Finn's harsh voice cut in, 'I'll see to her. We'll be lucky if she doesn't have a tantrum. You appear to have got her wildly over-excited.'

He reached down and extracted the wriggling little body from beneath the cot, taking charge, leaving Caro in no doubt at all that he believed that total mayhem would ensue if the apology for a nanny had anything more to do with his daughter.

'Get dressed and packed,' he instructed tersely as, the squirming baby tucked safely under one arm, he moved around the room selecting everything he'd need. Then he exited, presumably to use his own *en suite* again, and left Caro standing there feeling strangely breathless and utterly, utterly useless.

But, true to form, she soon had her brain back into gear, packed methodically, making sure Horn went in with Sophie's things, and then showered briefly. She put on a straight-cut navy cotton skirt and a short-sleeved white shirt, brushed her hair until it was exactly as neat as it should be and dabbed on moisturiser and the minimum of pale pink lipstick.

She looked capable and sensible, even if Finn Helliar thought she wasn't. Last night she had had the definite impression that he was flirting with her, testing the water so to speak. But if she'd got it wrong—and she could have done—and the sultry tone in his voice, the intimate gleam in his eyes had been all in her imagination, then he would surely sack her for gross incompetence and ask the agency to supply another temporary nanny.

She had proved herself to be spectacularly useless and by now any other employer would have been giving her her marching orders. For the next few days he would have no need of a nanny in any case.

He was good with the baby, knew what he was doing, and stuck in a country cottage he wouldn't be around for heavy dates with the sultry Sandra, so having someone on hand to child-mind wouldn't be a factor.

If he was a caring, responsible husband and father he would tell her to get lost.

If he was Finn Helliar, user of women, betrayer and deceiver, and fancied a bit of a fling with the new nanny, he would do no such thing.

The next half an hour or so would tell.

It did. An hour later the gleaming new off-roader had left the city behind, heading up the motorway, the baby safely strapped in her seat.

She'd had everything she meant to say to him about his immoral treatment of Katie ready to trip off her tongue the moment he told her to take her packed bags and get out. But she'd had to swallow them. Because the moment she'd stepped out of her room the easy charm of his smile had told her his black mood had gone.

'Ready?' His silver eyes had been sultrily hooded, thick dark lashes hiding his true expression as he'd submitted her suddenly quivering body to a long, lazy scrutiny. And when his eyes had at last made contact with hers there had been a gleam in them she definitely hadn't liked.

'There was no need to go to such stark lengths to

make amends for your earlier hoydenish behaviour...and appearance...'

His voice had lingered over the last two words, as if he was recalling every detail, savouring with hindsight the way she must have looked, crawling over the floor clad only in a faded old T-shirt that had probably exposed more essentials than it had covered.

He'd been referring to the way she was dressed now, of course, and she couldn't think how to answer him, much less quell him. It had been difficult to think at all when the inside of her head was in such a mess, brains scrambled, trying to decide what was best to do.

He didn't seem about to sack her for gross incompetence, which proved her earlier theories right, which, in turn, meant that spending a few days alone with him in some cosy little rustic retreat would be like walking into the lion's den!

So maybe, she'd thought, it would be best to come right out with it all now, tell him exactly what she thought of him, make him see the damage he'd done, make him understand that if David Parker, her grandmother's head gardener, hadn't been young and fit, and coincidentally on hand, Katie would have been successful in her broken-hearted attempt to drown herself in the deep black waters of that isolated lake on the family estate.

And then she could walk out, get on with her real life, and never have to have anything to do with the pernicious Casanova again, the anger and outrage at what he'd done finally vented from her system.

Best for her, maybe. Yet if she was brave enough there was another way, one that had flashed tantalisingly into her mind. An insane idea and she wouldn't give it headroom so why had she heard herself telling him, 'Yes, I'm ready.'?

'I'm afraid the second bedroom's rather cramped,' Finn found himself apologising. 'My friends, Ben and his wife Joanna, have two boys—a four-year-old and a baby of nine months—hence the cot and narrow single. But if you feel cramped and uncomfortable we'll swap rooms.' He picked Sophie up off the floor and settled her against his hip, his eyes intent on his companion.

Caroline Farr was quite a lady. Clearly out of her depth in the situation she'd plunged into, yet just as clearly determined to hang onto it. Quite unlike her sister Katie, this one was a fighter.

When he'd first met Katie at her grandmother's eightieth birthday party she'd seemed like a bunch of fresh spring flowers in a cupboardful of dusty old aspidistras and it had soon become painfully obvious that she had the habit of trying to become invisible when in her grandmother's company.

Elinor was an overpowering old lady and only respected those who stood up to her. He had felt desperately sorry for the appealingly pretty young girl and one thing had led to another and he'd ended up in a situation that had been problematical, to say the least.

There would be no such difficulties with Caro. She was a different breed entirely. No clinging vine...

'The room's fine,' she answered primly, staring at the pretty flower-sprigged cotton curtains at the dormer window, wondering what she thought she was doing here.

Then she remembered precisely what she thought she was doing here and went cold all over, frantically debating whether she had what it took to get the game moving.

'Right, if you're sure about that I'll leave you to unpack. But remember the offer's there if you change your mind. And perhaps you could make up the beds while I take Sophie down to explore the garden? We'll go to the village for provisions when you're ready.' He turned in the doorway. 'And get out of that prison-warder outfit while you're about it.' He grinned at her, hoping to put her at her ease.

She'd been subdued since he'd bawled her out for racketing around with the baby early this morning, his anger a direct reaction to the sudden, almost overwhelming need to scoop her up into his arms and kiss her silly.

But she had no way of knowing that, of course, and now he had to put her at ease, or as much at ease as the poor sweet would ever be until she came clean and told him exactly why she was pretending to be a nanny.

She was an independent young woman and if only half of what her grandmother had said about her was true she was intelligent, highly motivated and intensely loyal. He knew she wouldn't tell him a thing until he'd gained her trust.

He was going to get working on it, in earnest.

Alone, Caro sank down on the edge of the bed. She was suffering the unnerving experience of despising herself. All through her life she'd made her own decisions and, once made, she'd stuck to them, gone flat out to attain her goals.

Yet she was dithering over this one. It wasn't like her to be so feeble. Part of her brain was telling her to carry out her plan to hit that ratfink where it hurt before telling him exactly who she was and why she had suffered his odious company for so long, telling him exactly what he had done to Katie.

The other part was telling her to cut and run. Pick up her suitcase and walk down those stairs, phone for a taxi, give the brute a piece of her mind and get back to safety.

That was what was bugging her—the safety bit. She instinctively knew that if she stuck to her game plan she would be putting herself in danger.

Already that abundance of charm of his was getting to her, and there were some things about the wretch that she actually liked—his moments of consideration for her, the care and devotion he showed to his daughter, the way he had of taking charge with a natural warmth and ease, not with the cold arrogance she'd hated in the few other wealthy and highly successful males she'd encountered.

And, unlike any of the other males she'd occasionally dated, Finn Helliar had something special going for him, something that reached deep inside her and found a responsive chord she hadn't known she possessed.

She wasn't ready to respond to any man, not in that way, least of all Finn Helliar. It would be dangerous to get more involved with him.

Yet she hated him, didn't she? Surely that should be safeguard enough?

Grinding her teeth with rage over her own lack of decision, she got to her feet and stamped over to the window, looking out, and wished she hadn't because Finn was there in the garden, hunkered down on the soft green grass, one hand steadying his baby, the other pointing to one of the heavily flowered rose bushes.

He was shaking his head, pointing to the bush, obviously teaching the child one of life's most salutary lessons. That roses have thorns.

He stood, clasping Sophie's small hand, and they continued their slow discovery of the garden, and Caro's stomach muscles contracted as her eyes swept the hard, wide lines of his shoulders, the taut narrowness of his waist and hips. And the way the denim fabric hugged his thighs made something stab painfully deep inside her.

She turned away, her fingers gripping the edge of the small chest of drawers, her eyes tightly closed as she fought to gain some control of her stupidly wayward senses.

She was mad to let the man's undoubted sex appeal get to her this way! He used that damned sensual charisma like a weapon and left bleeding hearts behind.

Why else should his wife of a mere two years be conspicuous by her absence, leaving him to make major decisions—hiring a nanny for their beautiful little daughter, choosing where they would live—if she weren't away somewhere, hurt and disenchanted?

And she only had to remember Katie, the vulnerability of her ashen face, the shadows of pain and distress in her haunted eyes, when she'd told her what had happened...

* * *

Caro had just settled into the new partnership and was putting the finishing touches to the flat in Highgate she'd moved into, relishing having her own space after sharing with two other students while she'd been doing her business studies course, when her mother phoned, sounding frantic.

'You must come home this weekend.'

An anxious frown pulled Caro's brows together. Her mother never insisted on anything; she was more than happy to allow everyone else to do their own thing, in their own way, because it made life much simpler. 'Is anything wrong?' She knew something must be.

'It's Katie. I can't get through to her, but you could. She listens to you. And I daren't tell your grandmother—you know what she's like.' It all came rushing out, like a torrent when a dam had been breached, the words almost tumbling over themselves. 'She's been in bed for days, ever since the accident—I thought it was an accident but now I'm not so sure. She won't get up. Just lies there. Won't eat. If I ask her what's wrong she says, ''Nothing,'' and turns her face to the wall. She won't look at me, or tell me anything. She's always crying. Say one word and she bursts into tears.'

'What accident?'

'She fell into Quarry Lake; at least that's what I assumed happened. If David Parker hadn't been in the vicinity and jumped in to pull her out, she never would have survived. She was always too afraid of water to learn to swim properly.'

Caro gave an involuntary shudder. The lake, the site of a long-abandoned quarry on the northern rim of the family estate, was a sinister place; the tree-hung area always seemed cold, even in mid-summer, the still waters dark and deep.

'She's probably still in shock,' she told her mother reassuringly. 'Do try not to worry. I'll drive down this afternoon and if she's not showing signs of getting back to normal by the morning we'll call the doctor in and get him to check her over.'

Privately thinking her parent should have consulted Dr Grice immediately after the accident, Caro aborted her plans for enjoying her new flat this weekend and drove home. Ever since she'd been around ten years old and had developed a mind of her own, she'd been making most of the decisions for her family, as well as defending them against the sharp tongue of her grandmother.

Gran called her daughter-in-law and younger grandchild simpering fools and only tolerated their presence in the lodge because she could keep an eye on them, tell them what to do, keeping a tight hold on the family purse-strings, keeping them dependent because, as Caro suspected, it gave her a sense of power.

Springing to her small family's defence, Caro had coldly pointed out that her mother and sister were not fools, simpering or otherwise. They were sweet-natured, both of them. Shy but loving. And terrified of her. And who in their right mind wouldn't be?

'You, for one!' the old lady had snorted, her faded eyes approving. 'I've never been afraid of anything in my life. You're a chip off the old block, I'm relieved to say!'

Caro devoutly hoped she wasn't. True, she knew

what she wanted and went all out to get it, but she hoped she would never develop into such a cantankerous old biddy!

Smiling ruefully, she pulled up on the drive of the lodge, confident that Katie was suffering nothing worse than the aftermath of falling into the lake, a place she had always avoided when they'd been children together roaming the estate. She must at least have got rid of some of her childhood antipathy to the area to have chosen to walk there...

For once her confidence was misplaced. Katie looked even worse than their mother had intimated. Alone with her, Caro opened the bedroom curtains, letting in the sunlight, and Katie flinched, hiding her face in her hands, turning her head away.

Consciously trying not to frown worriedly, Caro sat on the edge of her sister's bed and said gently, 'Mum told me you had an accident—fell in the lake of all places!' And she had all the breath knocked out of her body when Katie launched herself at her, clinging, holding her tight, sobbing as if her heart would break.

'Hey!' Caro said softly when the storm at last died down. 'What's all this about, sweetie? So you fell in the water, and that would have been a shock, but Dave was on hand to pull you out, so no harm done.' She smiled reassuringly, but Katie wouldn't have seen that because her head was bowed. 'I can only suggest that if you go for a walk in the direction of the lake again you take Dave with you! He's so nice, don't you think?' Gently, she tucked her fingers beneath her sister's chin, forcing her to look at her. And what she saw appalled her.

Although Katie had had her eighteenth birthday

only a few short weeks ago, her eyes had always been childishly wide and innocent. Now they looked old, weary beyond measure, shadowed by dark circles, her once smoothly pretty cheeks fallen in, making her look gaunt, her peaches-and-cream complexion a dismaying ash-grey.

'I don't care if Dave rescued me. No big deal.' Tears brimmed her eyes again. 'I don't care if I went in the water—don't you understand? I don't care about anything. Not now. Not ever again!'

Ice closed around Caro's heart. 'Is that your way of saying it wasn't an accident? You didn't find yourself down at the lakeside by mistake, and somehow tumble in?'

Katie lifted her head and looked at her blankly, then lowered her eyes, muttering almost inaudibly, 'What do you think?'

Caro didn't know what to think but she wasn't going to say so. Instead she asked, 'Can you tell me why you can't care about anything?'

'I loved him. I thought he loved me,' she answered quaveringly. Shakily, she reached for the night table and took a piece of carefully folded newsprint from the drawer, holding it out. 'Then I saw this.'

It was a wedding shot. Caro scanned the accompanying text. A very eminent banker and his new bride. A very handsome banker by the name of Finn Helliar. The surname rang bells, but faintly. His lovely bride was Fleur Ferrand, a previously obscure French singer who had recently shot to public recognition.

'They're having a baby; it says so. Going to

live—live in Canada.' Katie's voice wobbled ominously.

'This is the man you thought you were in love with?'

'I didn't think I was. I was in love with him. I am in love with him,' Katie said on a reassuringly mutinous note, showing a smidgen of spirit at last, much to Caro's relief. 'And I truly believed he loved me. He was so kind, that day, you wouldn't believe. Oh, he did say he thought I was a bit young. After all, I was still only seventeen, but, like I told him, I was nearly eighteen and old enough to do what I wanted.'

'What day was that?' Caro asked as levelly as she could. What could a thirty-two-year-old successful banker be wanting with a seventeen-year-old virgin barely out of the schoolroom?

Silly question!

Tears brimmed and fell. 'The last day. The last day I saw him. He was going to be out of the country for a while. We were in his flat. He took me there,' she said ingenuously. 'My blouse was all torn. He couldn't have been sweeter. He even phoned through to his office and got his secretary to buy me a new one, and bring it round. He was the only person ever to make me feel special, and important—other than you and Mum, of course.'

'I'm going to fix us a hot drink.' Caro couldn't stay in the room a moment longer, not without giving vent to the red-hot anger that was consuming her.

'Don't want anything.' Katie was pleating the sheets in shaky fingers.

'Yes, you do. We both do. Then you can tell me more about it.'

Her mother caught up with her in the kitchen while she was heating milk for cocoa. Caro hated the stuff but would gladly drink gallons if only to persuade Katie to take the first nourishment she'd had for days, apparently.

'How is she?' Pretty and pale with anxiety, Emma Farr hovered in the doorway and Caro answered briskly.

'Not good, but she'll get better; just give it time. It's not the after-effects of tumbling into the lake.' No way would she confide that Katie had as good as admitted she'd tried to drown herself. 'Actually, she's suffering from a first love affair that went wrong.' The more innocuous she made it sound, the better her mother would be able to cope.

'Don't try to get her to talk about it; she'll tell you in her own good time. And what I suggest is that you take her on a long holiday, see new places and faces and have fun. I'll square the cost of it with Gran, and you'll both need new clothes. Lots of them. I'll square that, too. I'll make the bookings on Monday. A world cruise suit you? All you have to do is make sure your passports are up to date and drag Katie out to buy those new glad rags.'

It was difficult to persuade her sister to take that extended holiday, but she managed it. Nevertheless it took ages for the young girl to get back to her normal, sweetly contented self.

Finn Helliar had left scars that took a long time to heal. And Caro wasn't able to discover much more about the shameful affair. Katie was vague about how and where they'd met, saying it didn't matter—nothing mattered now, did it?

*   *   *

Caro opened her eyes, squeezed tightly closed for too long, as the familiar anger came surging back.

Finn Helliar was a louse. Seducing an innocent seventeen-year-old and walking away to marry the woman who was carrying his baby! And how sweet of him to go to the enormous trouble and expense of getting his secretary to replace the blouse he'd torn in his uncontrollable lust!

He would pay for that! And Caroline Farr knew exactly how she would make it happen!

CHAPTER FIVE

THE dazzling blue of the sky, coupled with the sheer brilliance of the midsummer sunlight, was such a contrast to the darkness of Caro's recent thoughts, it made her feel dizzy.

The sensual warmth of the sun on her bare arms, the caress of the light breeze as it moulded the soft, floaty cotton of her cream-coloured skirt around her legs and the scented freshness of the air all combined to make her poor head spin.

Or had the dizziness, the frightening feeling of not being in complete control, got something to do with the way Finn turned and looked at her as she walked—strangely hesitant now—down the path to where he stood on the curving lawn?

Just looked at her with that spine-prickling, breath-snagging expression in his smouldering silver eyes, straightening up slowly. The child was at his feet, contentedly playing with a handful of daisies, oblivious to the tension Caro could taste on every trembling breath of air she pulled into her lungs.

'Entrancing,' he murmured at last, his voice so low she wondered if she'd imagined the compliment on her appearance.

She wasn't wearing a nanny get-up, quite deliberately. Prison-warder outfits didn't fit the bill for what she had in mind. So she'd chosen this floaty, almost transparent skirt, a soft coffee-coloured camisole top and a pair of strappy sandals designed to emphasise the arch of her instep. And the height of the heels had to be responsible for the way her body seemed to sway...

'Thank you.' She even managed to smile, just a little. Managed to curb the impulse to run right out of his life, or tell him precisely what she thought of him. Doing either of those things would be a mistake and ruin the game before play had started.

'Let's investigate what the village stores have to offer in the way of provisions.' Finn lifted Sophie into his arms, pulled a daisy stalk out of her mouth and tilted an enquiring brow at the hired nanny who definitely looked good enough to eat.

It had been his sensible intention to suggest she stay here with his daughter, allowing them both the time to get to feel at home with the cottage and garden while he drove into the village to stock up with what they'd need for the next day or so.

But sense, it would appear, had flown out of sight. He didn't want to leave her behind. He wanted her with him. Because the question of why she was in his employ at all and inexpertly posing as a qualified nanny intrigued him? Or did it go further than that?

He knew darn well it went further than that.

'OK.' The smile she gave him was warm and winning and he caught his breath, wanting more, wanting to drown in the enticing fascination of that smile, but she turned, depriving him of the opportunity, and he followed her back along the path.

He locked the cottage door and strode across the gravel to the parked car. Sophie, now comfortably strapped into her seat, was about to fall asleep, and one of the loveliest young women he had ever had the good fortune to set eyes on was waiting for him in the passenger seat.

Life was good!

So, the day was good, his mood was better—no need at this stage to try to force the truth from her. Leave it. This was a day to be enjoyed, savoured, one of those perfect days the English summer came up with every now and then, and Caroline Farr—apparently discarding her prickles and suddenly in holiday mood—was too exquisitely entrancing to frighten away with pushy questions.

'I only hope the whole village doesn't close down at lunchtime!' A sideways smile into her eyes as he turned the key in the ignition met with a sudden, unexpected flash of wariness, a slight quick frown which was successfully hidden by the way she immediately swung her head round, staring out of the passenger window.

He frowned, his shrug negligible, a barely perceptible upward drift of his shoulders before he released the handbrake and drove the vehicle onto the narrow country lane at a carefully sober pace.

The relaxed holiday mood of hers hadn't lasted long. Pity. He would have enjoyed relaxing with her, drawing her out, getting to know her.

But something had obviously wound her up, made her regroup those prickly defences.

Had she become suddenly conscious of letting go, of actually enjoying the day and the company, then, because of that, become fearful that she might be unwary enough to confess whatever troubles had brought her into his employ in the first place? Only time and patience on his part would tell.

'If the village shops prove hopeless I'll try further afield.' As soon as that spineless inanity was out of his mouth Finn could have bitten his tongue off. He sounded like an old woman, harping on about provisions and shopping! It wasn't the sort of conversation he wanted to have with her at all!

'I'm sure that won't be necessary. We're not going to be around for long so I guess we can survive on the basics.' Caro forced herself to speak lightly even though her throat was tightening, her pulses thudding. Her stupid heart had leapt like a landed fish, her whole body and mind panicking, when he'd smiled into her eyes back there.

Panicking because, much as she would like to be able to, she couldn't deny the way her wretched body had responded to those wicked, come-to-bed eyes.

Although the whole object of the exercise was to give him the impression that that was exactly what was happening to her, it had to be make-believe, not sickeningly terrifying reality!

She dared not come anywhere near responding to him in any way—except in revulsion and disgust and utter, utter contempt! Unfortunately, she was unusually vulnerable as far as he was concerned. It meant she had to be permanently on her guard.

She gave him a contrived wide-eyed look, horribly aware of the rapid, suffocating beats of her heart. 'If it would help I'll cope with the catering while we're here, and leave you free to house-hunt, or whatever.'

Didn't they say the way to a man's heart was through his stomach? And wasn't she a great cook?

She barely knew one end of a baby from another but she knew her way around a kitchen. If all else failed she could try to grab his interest via her culinary skills.

'Catering, viewing properties—whatever, I'd rather we did everything together.'

Lightly spoken but an order nevertheless. It kept her silent while he negotiated the narrow high street. The tone of his voice had been an unveiled caress. It sent shivers down her spine.

Fear, distaste, whatever. One thing she did now know: if she returned the right signals the game would be on.

She waited until he'd parked in the shade of one of the oak trees that bordered the village green, then gathered up all of her courage and lightly touched his bare forearm with the tips of her fingers.

'Everything?' The firm vibrancy of the flesh beneath her fingertips made her pulses flutter; the instinctive tightening of those honed muscles and tendons in preparation for action made her throat close up with fright. At least she didn't have to work at sounding husky! She hated touching him. She wanted to snatch her hand away.

Forcing herself to keep control, she made herself add, 'Sounds—interesting,' and eased her fingers gently away from that tanned male flesh, knowing the game was on as speculation changed to triumphant male certainty in the deep silver pools of his eyes.

But he didn't push it; at least he wasn't crass enough to do that. She had to be grateful for small mercies. The flicker of awareness, of male certainty, had been compelling, unarguable.

She'd given him the signals he'd been looking for, the green light that told him she was willing.

The game was on.

Nothing happened.

Caro wished with all her heart that it would. She pushed a hand through her hair, mussing it wildly. The tension of waiting for something to happen was far worse than coping with it when it did.

Sophie, tucked up in her cot, was sleeping the sleep of the totally innocent and Caro, feeling far from innocent, glared at her reflection in the mirror and knew she had to try harder.

Either she and Finn were working to a different set of rules and she'd been mistaken about those signals, or he'd completely lost all interest.

They'd shopped, they'd eaten, they'd made the cross-country journey to the first property he had arranged to view and Finn Helliar had behaved like a perfect gentleman throughout.

Which under normal circumstances would have been fine, exactly right and as it should be between employer and employee.

But these weren't normal circumstances. She needed him to make an advance of some kind so that she could respond and lead him on, let him believe she was eager for the sort of hole-and-corner affair he thrived on. And then, when he was all fired up, slap him down and walk away, only pausing long enough to ask him if he liked the feeling of being dumped.

'I'll put a salad together and barbecue a couple of steaks,' he'd told her after they'd bathed the baby and put her down to sleep. And now the smell of chargrilled meat was drowning out the evening scents of roses and honeysuckle, making her feel sick.

Or did that feeling of nausea spring from nervous tension? A fastidious distaste for the way she had chosen? Whatever. She only had to remind herself of what he'd done to Katie to get herself back on track.

The gauzy bedroom drapes were billowing gently in the soft evening breeze. She lifted them slightly to one side. She could see him moving about on the paved terrace below, putting a bowl, plates, wine and glasses down on the teak picnic-style table.

Her stomach lurched. She was going to have to try harder, tempt him to make a move. She didn't have time to waste because in another thirty-six hours or so they'd be back in London and as soon as they were she wouldn't hang around. She'd be back to the agency faster than he could blink, mission accomplished.

After bathing she'd wrapped herself in a silky, thigh-length robe. She could stay that way, barefoot and naked apart from wispy blue silk secured by a loosely tied sash, if only she were brave enough. But she wasn't.

Impatient with herself, she pulled on a pair of very short shorts and topped them with a toning pale amber top. Cropped and sleeveless, it looked much less workmanlike with most of the covered buttons left carelessly undone.

By twisting and peering she could see most of herself in the small tilting mirror on top of the narrow chest of drawers. With the limited choice of clothes she had with her she'd achieved the desired effect.

Sexy and sensual without looking cheap or up for grabs. It was the best she could do.

She decided to stay bare-footed, left her normally sleek bob mussed, ignored the contents of her make-up bag, checked on the blissfully sleeping baby one last time and, scarcely daring to breathe, trailed the back of her fingers gently over the rosy cheeks.

A wave of tenderness turned her heart to mush. She could hardly believe the speed with which this delightful child had become so important to her. She wished she could wave a magic wand and turn the baby's father into a faithful husband, bring her missing mummy back from wherever she was and give the child the precious gift of a happy family life. Then she silently berated herself for being such a sentimental fool.

She had no magic wand. The only thing she could do to help change Sophie's daddy's attitude to women was give him a taste of his own medicine. Then, if he experienced the misery and humiliation of being used and dumped, he might stop doing it to other people.

Caro braced herself then padded silently down the twisty stairs to try her reluctant hand at the flirting game.

CHAPTER SIX

CARO walked quickly out onto the terrace. Her courage would desert her entirely if she stopped to actually think about what she was doing.

Although she was sure her bare-footed approach had been completely silent Finn was obviously aware of her presence. He didn't turn from the barbecue he was working with but he knew she was there because he remarked evenly, 'Why don't you help yourself to wine? There's a bottle on the table. The steaks won't take much longer.'

Caro pulled in a deep shuddering breath. She didn't know why she looked on his instruction as a reprieve, the excuse she needed to make herself invisible, but she did. That reaction made her hands shake as she lifted the wine bottle from the cooler, made the neck of the bottle clatter against the rim of the glass as she poured.

The obvious thing to do, given the dubious role she had taken on, was to pour him some of the chilled white wine too, carry it over, talk to the man while he was cooking their supper, smile, pout, gaze into his eyes and bat her eyelashes—whatever—whatever it took to signal her willingness to play games.

But she couldn't bring herself to do any of those things. She wanted to run and hide because the height of him, the breadth of his back, the daunting width of his shoulders all suddenly intimidated her. At least, she was as certain as she could be that that was what was giving her the shakes.

Her eyes wide and wary, fixedly staring at the back of his dark and handsome head, she sidled silently over the paved terrace and down to the curving lawn until, out of sight, she sank cross-legged on the cool green grass and drained the contents of her glass in one long, recklessly thirsty swallow.

'You looked as if you needed that!' The husky, slightly gravelly voice was threaded through with strands of amusement and Caro flinched at his unexpected and unwanted appearance, squeezing her eyes tightly shut as he lowered himself to the ground beside her. Close beside her.

Alcohol fizzed through her veins. Or was it the needle-sharp awareness of how close his body was to hers? Of how scantily clad she was?

'Here, have mine.' Finn exchanged the full glass he'd carried down with him for her empty one. Their fingers brushed. Caro took a sharp breath and her eyes batted open, fastening with unwilling fascination on his sensual mouth, on that barely discernible slow, wicked shadow of a smile.

She didn't really want more wine, but took the glass because holding it gave her something to do, taking unthinking sips of the crisp, cool liquid until she realised she'd slurped her way through half the contents in less than a couple of minutes. She put the glass down quickly on the grass. Was he trying to get her drunk, incapable of knowing what she was doing? Was that the way he operated?

Having satisfied himself that she was willing to play along, he had done nothing more about it until his daughter was safely asleep for the night. That made sense, she supposed. But what happened now? Get her drunk and incapable, cutting out the tiresome need to sweet-talk her or the chore of having to make some pretence of caring about her, then jump on her?

Wham, bam and thank you, ma'am, and I won't say anything if you won't; it can be our little secret and don't tell the wife?

Oh, how debauched and utterly, utterly despicable! Oh, how she hated him! And was ready to punch him if he so much as touched her!

He didn't. He said, 'Let's go and eat,' and got effortlessly to his feet, casually holding a hand out to her.

Caro took it because the only other option she had was to crawl back up to the terrace on her hands and knees. Suddenly her head was spinning wildly. Every nerve in her body tingled as those hard, warm fingers closed reassuringly around her own and the sensual shock of the sensation was responsible for the way her fingers clung so desperately to his; of course it was. And she clung even more tightly as he bent to retrieve their glasses.

And when he straightened up her body inadvertently swayed giddily towards his, brushed against the taut, lean length of him, the tips of her suddenly unbearably sensitised breasts grazing the soft dark cotton that covered his deep chest.

'Oh!' Caro gasped then trembled violently, every cell in her body leaping in hectic response to the tough, masculine feel of him, the warmth of him, the closeness of him. Unnamed emotions—dozens of them—surged frantically around inside her; she was so confused she didn't know what to do with herself. Cling to him and wrap her arms tightly around him, or take to her heels and run a mile?

Wrapping her arms around his neck and pulling his head down to hers, pressing her tingling body even closer to his could be one of her better ideas—in the cause of her ultimate revenge, of course.

However, running the proverbial mile would put her out of danger. But surely there was no danger at all? There shouldn't be, not as long as she played the seduction game by her own private set of rules!

But would she remember the rules? Her body, wriggling closer into his right now, at this very moment, seemed to have forgotten there had ever been any!

Confusion reigned.

'Steady!' With a wry, lop-sided grin as he capitulated to a surge of unexpected chivalry, Finn managed to hold onto the wine glasses, prise his daughter's nanny's delectably curvy, inviting little body from all over his and steer them both in the direction of the terrace and the waiting steaks which would undoubtedly be as hard as leather and stone-cold by now.

The way she'd fallen against him, her fantastic body wriggling and clinging, had been out-of-this-world provocation. Finn wondered if it could have been deliberate—like the way she'd disappeared to the far end of the garden, practically inviting him to follow. Or whether her unsteadiness had been a result of swallowing her wine far too quickly.

He gave her the benefit of the doubt and put the sexually provocative moment down to the wine. His hand was on the small of her back because he suspected she was ever so slightly tipsy and he didn't want her to fall over her feet.

He would prefer not to have to touch her, not under these circumstances. Touching her put far too much strain on his self-control. Stone-cold sober and fully aware of what she was doing—now that would be another story altogether.

Finn pulled his mind sharply away from that enticing scenario, guided her to the picnic table and went to collect the meat.

He wanted to touch her, to hold her, wanted it with a sharp, compelling urgency he hadn't experienced in a very long time, probably not since adolescence and rioting hormones had driven him into the wholehearted exploration of the mysteries of the female sex.

And when he finally took her in his arms he wanted her fully aware of what was happening, crystal-clear about the consequences of the step they would be taking. He wouldn't want her mental and physical faculties blurred by an injudicious intake of alcohol.

Besides, there was another, more altruistic side to his interest in this endlessly fascinating woman. He wanted to get to know why she was having to pretend to be a nanny in order to earn a few extra bucks, and she wouldn't confide in him until she could trust him, and she sure as hell wouldn't trust him if he gave way to his suddenly rampaging male hormones, dragged her into his arms and covered every inch of her face and body with hungry, burning kisses.

It was too soon. Much too soon. True, she was older, more sophisticated and far less naive than her younger sister had been, and the gasp of excited response she'd given when she'd stumbled against him, their bodies brushing, touching and burning from breast to thigh, had told him she was just as sexually aware of him as he was of her.

Even so, he wasn't going to rush a thing. Instinct told him that their future relationship could be interesting. More than merely interesting. He wouldn't risk putting it in jeopardy through lack of patience.

Fortunately the meat hadn't been ruined by the delay and the salad was absolutely fine, and as he helped himself to wine after she'd shaken her head and covered her glass with her hand in refusal she remarked, 'You cook a mean steak.' Reluctant humour lit her eyes. 'Why is it that men see tending a barbecue as a perfectly acceptable masculine activity but wouldn't be seen dead anywhere near a kitchen stove and a potato-peeler?'

'Don't generalise.' His eyes glinted at her over the rim of his glass. 'They don't come much better than me around the kitchen stove—or sink, for that matter. I have been known to rise from Sophie's strained vegetables to a four-course dinner for six, believe it or not.'

She might believe it; at a pinch she just might. Not because she thought he was incapable of lying—he had done nothing but lie to poor Katie—or because his lazy grin was totally disarming and unbelievably sexy, but because, for all he was by all accounts as rich as Croesus, he didn't flaunt his great wealth.

The property she, at his insistence, had viewed with him this afternoon had positively reeked of wealth and perfect taste. Ultra-modern, enclosed in acres of beautifully manicured grounds, the house had boasted every luxury and convenience known to man—discreetly boasted, of course. She had privately thought that the place would suit him very well, that he'd lose no time in getting his solicitor to exchange contracts.

But Finn, guiding Sophie through the great sliding glass doors that led from the airy book room into a huge domed space-age conservatory, had observed, 'Very avant-garde, but not exactly homely. Can't see us romping here, can you, Sophie, girl?'

So yes, unfortunately she could bring herself to believe he was as handy around a kitchen as he was with his baby daughter. She wished she couldn't believe anything good or halfway human about him. She wanted to hate him through and through, not grudgingly have to respect bits of his character.

But there was no point in letting her emotions get in the way here. So, he had his good points, but that did nothing to alter what he'd done to Katie.

He was leaning forward now, his tanned forearms on the rough, grainy surface of the wooden picnic table, idly twisting the stem of his glass between those long, strong fingers. She couldn't read his expression, not clearly, because the daylight was fading rapidly now, but his voice was warm, intimate, as he invited, 'Tell me about yourself, Caro.'

As an opener it sounded promising. However, she had no intention of telling him anything about herself, not yet anyway, not until she was ready to tell him whose sister she was; so she manufactured what she hoped would pass as a seductive smile and disclaimed huskily, 'I'm sure we could find something far less boring to talk about. You, for instance—'

'Not at all.' Finn stretched out his long legs beneath

the table and told her, 'As a topic of conversation I'm sure I'd find you endlessly fascinating.'

And wasn't that the truth? The way she'd smiled at him just now had been a definite come-on, completely at odds with the wary, almost frightened look in her eyes. Almost as if she was flirting with him, inviting him to come close, to touch, but would head for the hills if he so much as moved a muscle!

He smiled at her, trying to put her at her ease, wanting her to open up. If she and her agency were having problems then there was a strong possibility he could help. He wanted to help her, and not entirely because of the family business connection, either; he could be completely honest with himself on that score. 'How about telling me why you chose looking after other people's children as a profession?' he suggested. 'Have you always been a nanny?'

In the waning light her skin gleamed like ivory, the cropped top she was wearing displaying her neat midriff and the slender length of her neck and arms, the dusky valley between her breasts tantalisingly on view because of the number of artfully unfastened buttons.

Desire stirred roughly—an instant, predictable and ungovernable reaction to one very sexy lady!

Caro's eyes widened in consternation as she watched the way he suddenly shifted uncomfortably on his seat, the way the lines at the corners of his mouth hardened, and cast desperately around for something to say.

The flirting game seemed to have been going well. She didn't want his mood to change to impatience, and by the look of things it was doing just that, but she couldn't answer his questions, either.

She gulped. Things were getting scary. Maybe she should give him one last chance to redeem himself. She would casually mention his wife, the missing Fleur, and judge his reaction. If he explained why she wasn't around, and the explanation was reasonable and nothing like her own wild and dark imaginings, then she would revise her opinion and mark his flirtatious behaviour down to harmless habit.

But if he tried to tell her that his wife didn't understand him, or wasn't too important in his life, then she would know the leopard hadn't changed his spots and would have to move in for the kill.

'Surely you won't be able to make a decision on your future home without having Mrs Helliar's opinion?' There, despite the way he had never once, in any connection, mentioned his absent wife, her question, in the circumstances, would seem perfectly natural. She watched his face for any signs of awkwardness but he merely smiled dismissively, lifting those wide, hard shoulders in a lazy shrug.

'Why on earth would you think that? As she'll never spend more than one month in twelve in the UK she'd be the first to agree that her opinion on mine and Sophie's future home was irrelevant. Now, shall I make coffee, or will you?'

He had had his chance to redeem himself, and failed. His message was clear. He and his wife were as good as separated. He could do as he liked. His wife's opinion didn't count.

It was now time for action, not words, she decided feverishly. And, although her heart was racing, by a supreme effort of will she made her movements slow and slinky as she got to her feet and stretched languorously, her hands loosely clasped behind her head.

'No coffee for me, thanks. I'm going to amble around the garden. After that steak, I've got a feeling I could do with the exercise.'

She lowered her arms quickly. The way his eyes made a slow journey of discovery over the contour lines of her body made her stomach clench, the ferocity of the spasm taking her by surprise, making her voice sound as if it had been put through a grater as she invited belatedly, 'Coming?' and turned, swaying slowly over the terrace, one half of her hoping he'd take her up on the invitation and follow, the other half desperately praying he wouldn't.

He had caught up with her by the time she'd negotiated the shallow flight of steps that led down to the lawn. 'Watch where you're going!' Dusk was gathering, shadows deepening, drawing together. Her narrow, naked feet glimmered palely against the grass. 'There could be stones lying around. You might cut yourself.' An inane remark if ever there was one, made to cover the overwhelming impulse he had to lift her into his arms, carry her to his bed and make love to her until she knew darn well she belonged to him.

What the hell was he thinking of? Of course she didn't belong to him! He didn't know where the insane idea had come from—normal male lust for a ravishingly attractive woman didn't usually turn him into a fool, for pity's sake! Yet was it so foolish, so impossible?

He cleared his throat of some annoying constriction. 'We need to talk, Caroline. We really do.' It was way past time he levelled with her, told her—among other things—that he knew who she was. Get all that stuff out of the way, cards on the table, and then get on to what he darn well knew was a growing mental and physical attraction for him and, he suspected, for her, too.

Her feet shuffled to a halt, her toes curling in the cool green grass. Saying her name in full like that made everything seem more serious somehow. And talking wasn't on her agenda.

She flinched as he placed his hands on either side of her waist. The touch of his skin on the bare flesh of her midriff sent a massive shock wave through her, paralysing her. She couldn't say a word; only the faintest of moans escaped her parted lips when the pressure of those beautifully crafted hands increased as they tugged her into the lean strength of his body.

His body heat was drugging. She couldn't move, could only drift closer into him, her breath sobbing in her lungs as he made a growling noise in his throat—as if he had lost patience with himself, or her, or both of them—then brought his head down to take her parted lips with the sensual insistence of his.

As a kiss it was intense and primal, her fevered, instinctive response making her realise at last what desire was, how one particular man could set the senses soaring, how passion could leave the most upright woman alive contemplating moral bankruptcy!

Caro didn't know what was wrong with her. She was supposed to get him burning for her, not the other way around!

CHAPTER SEVEN

CARO woke to the sound of Sophie doing her best to out-sing the dawn chorus.

'Wow, and aren't we the early riser!' Caro hoisted herself up on one elbow and brushed her hair out of her eyes with the back of her hand. Six a.m. and the baby was wide awake, bright as a button, and her nanny, although she had hardly slept at all, had slept alone, and for that she had to be very, very thankful.

Because at one stage of the proceedings it had seemed almost a foregone conclusion that she would be sharing the double in the master bedroom. A kind of madness had overtaken her and she went hot and shaky all over now just remembering.

As his hands had begun a lazy exploration of her back, sliding beneath her top, stroking down over her shoulder blades then curving around her ribcage, the restless heat of passion had flamed fiercely inside her, driving her to press herself against his aroused body, everything inside her melting, shaking with need as he'd whispered thickly against her quivering mouth, 'See what you do to me? Stop me if this is too soon for you, but do it now, while I'm still capable of using some self-control.'

The balls of his thumbs had been describing soft circles on the underswell of both of her suddenly desperately aching breasts and she'd wanted him to make love to her, wanted it as she'd never wanted anything

82

before, and the self-betrayal would have been complete if those words of his hadn't finally got through the dizzily spinning remnants of her mind.

Something had frozen inside her. She was sure her heart had stopped beating. She'd snatched at the escape route he had offered and pushed out shakily, 'You're right. It is too soon…much too soon…I'm sorry, Finn…' And she'd jerked away from him, walking back towards the cottage on legs that felt decidedly tottery, not daring to look at him because if she had and he'd held out his hands and spoken her name she would have hurled herself back into his arms, all wisdom gone, her integrity in shreds. Such was the power of what he did to her.

And because the warm dark night had been still and silent Caro had heard the harshly painful intake of his breath but had made herself ignore it. So he was hurting—well, so was she—but, for pity's sake, she had been a whisper away from making love with a married man! The very thought gave her the moral shudders.

What type of alchemist was he, for goodness' sake? How black was the darkness of the spell he had cast?

Blinking rapidly, she pushed herself out of bed, away from her shameful recollections, and found a smile of sorts for his delightful baby.

'OK, sweetheart, if you promise to be quiet about it, we'll have a bath and start our day,' Caro promised in a husky whisper as she lifted the bright-eyed child from her cot. 'We don't want to wake Daddy, do we?'

Heaven forbid! Six o'clock in the morning was far too early to have to face him. She needed time to get her head together. One thing she did know, she assured herself as she plopped Sophie down on the floor while she collected up fresh day clothes for them both: things had to be brought to a head very soon.

She wanted it over. She needed it to be over. She wanted to get her life back.

Besides, the game she was playing was beginning to look scary. She was beginning to like him, to enjoy being around him, despite all the rotten things she knew about his character.

And worse, much, much worse, she had enjoyed having him touch her, caress her body, kiss her, and to her eternal shame she had wanted very much more. Something had happened when he'd held her in his arms—the birth of an elemental sexual chemistry that made her forget who he was and what he was, and why she was here. And that wasn't part of her game plan.

So the sooner everything was brought to a head the better, she reminded herself, hurrying her charge through the ritual of bathing and dressing, making sure what noise they made was as muted as possible.

'Shall we have breakfast in the garden?' Caro whispered as she carried Sophie to the head of the twisty stairs. She was going to have to flirt with Finn all day, lead him to believe she was just dying to jump into his bed, but she wanted some respite—she deserved some respite; besides, she'd walked away, hadn't she, told him it was all happening too soon?

Now she was going to have to convince him she'd had second thoughts and couldn't wait—she had all that work to do over again!

'Da-da, Da-da, Da-deee—!' Sophie's sudden, ecstatic shrieks made Caro feel ill with nervous tension.

She had hoped so desperately that he wouldn't wake for at least another hour.

After the intimacy of that physical encounter last night the thought of coming face to face with him again was deeply embarrassing. As the baby strained against her, holding her arms out to her father, Caro turned reluctantly and felt her face go red.

Finn Helliar was obviously on his way to the bathroom she and Sophie had recently vacated. Finn Helliar was almost naked. Cotton boxer shorts did nothing to detract from the masculine grace of that perfect body. Big-boned and strong, he carried no surplus flesh. Just looking at him made Caro's mouth go dry.

'Mornin', girls.' He looked aggravatingly relaxed—far too relaxed to have spent the night twitching and pillow-punching the way she had—his eyes a sleepy silver gleam. Or was that sleepy look due to lust? Could well be, Caro decided, her heart giving a sickening thump as those slumberous eyes slid lazily up and down the length of her shorts-and-T-shirt-clad body.

He took a step towards them, leaning forward to drop loving kisses on his little daughter's rosy cheek, and this close Caro could see every pore on his firm, tanned skin, the tiny laughter-lines at the corner of his eyes, the length of those thickly curving black lashes, the hard sweep of his stubble-darkened jaw.

This close. Almost as close as they'd been last night when he'd kissed her, stroked her disgracefully willing body. Close, intimately so. And just for a few breathless moments, as he leant forward to kiss the child she held in her arms, it felt as if they were a single entity, his hand resting lightly on her shoulder completing the circle. Inexplicably, for some remote and crazy reason, it made her want to cry.

'Did I hear you say something about breakfast in the garden? Sounds good to me. Toast and coffee will do for me. Ten minutes?'

He stepped back and the illusion of family intimacy was gone, the vacuum filled by another type of intimacy altogether. Elemental sexual desire glinted in his eyes as they transmitted a silent, timeless message deep into her own, making her body go limp and boneless, making her flesh ache for him.

Then it was gone, for him at least, gone in the flash of a wide white smile as he turned slowly away, the lean, spare breadth of his shoulders very effectively underlining his male dominance, the power he must know he held over her senses, leaving her trembling because that elemental desire was still there for her; for her it hadn't gone at all.

Not trusting her shaky legs to support her and the baby, Caro put Sophie down on her plump little legs, and, holding hands tightly, they bumped down the twisty staircase on their bottoms, giggling wildly, making a game of it.

An undignified but safe descent, and with Sophie crawling around her feet in the cute but cramped kitchen the makings of breakfast were quickly assembled—more quickly than her return to a state of equilibrium, a state she had barely and precariously achieved when Finn entered the tiny room and sent her senses haywire all over again.

He was dressed in lightweight, stone-coloured, narrow-fitting trousers and a collarless black cotton shirt, his dark hair curling damply into the nape of his neck, and his pervasive masculinity overwhelmed her all over again, plunging her straight back to square one.

She felt shattered and stupid—too stupid to do more than swallow convulsively when he gave the tray she'd loaded with Sophie's cereal and orange juice and coffee and toast for the adults the once-over and told her, 'I'll take it out. Bring Sophie, would you?'

She did as she was told, like a good little nanny, desperately wishing she didn't have to. She wanted out. Although she shouldn't be complaining, she reminded herself tartly; this farce was her idea. And the only way to get even the smallest amount of revenge was to stick to her plan.

'You know, I could get used to this.' Finn sat at the picnic table under a cloudless blue sky and took his daughter on his knee while Caro tipped cereal and milk into her bowl.

'Who couldn't? Until it rains—or winter comes!' She smiled, forcing herself to appear relaxed and natural. She poured coffee for herself and Finn and sat down opposite him and Sophie, cradling the steaming cup in both hands. 'But yes, it is a lovely morning and the garden's really pretty. I wonder how it's kept so nice—with the owners only coming here at weekends?'

She was babbling and she knew it, and he knew it too. She could tell he did by the way his eyes smiled into hers, his mouth curving into a slow, sexy smile.

'Someone from the village comes up once or twice a week and does the necessary, I believe,' he told her, his gaze drifting down to her mouth, lingering, and back to hold her eyes again. 'But I wasn't talking about our surroundings, or the glorious weather. I meant I could get used to the three of us being together.'

And what about your wife—you adulterous louse?

Caro swallowed the seething words with a mouthful of coffee. That reminder would come later, hopefully when he'd got to the point of believing the new nanny was his for the taking. Until then she had to smile sweetly and console herself with the knowledge that before either of them was very much older he too would know the pain and humiliation of being dumped!

She passed him the toast, wondering how a guy who looked so good on the outside could be rotten where it really mattered. He was a deceiver, a philanderer, and that made him ugly.

She ignored his hateful comment and managed to ask him smoothly, 'Are you viewing both the remaining properties today? Are we all going? And, if so, should I pack a picnic, or won't that be necessary?' Tilting her head on one side, she looked at him through lowered lashes, hoping to give him the impression that last night's 'too soon' could be today's 'maybe'.

The look he gave her was intense. His mouth tightened momentarily, as if he was about to say something of great significance, and then his wide shoulders visibly relaxed beneath the soft black cotton as he said, merely, 'Of course we're all going. I'll value your opinion. I'll pack some soft drinks and fruit in the cool-box if you'll get Sophie's things together.'

*   *   *

'I'm not going to have to look any further!'

The house named, strangely, Mytton Wells, was perfect. Finn knew he could search for a hundred years and still not find anything better as a home for Sophie to grow up in. And the strips of woodland and the flower-filled meadows that enclosed the house and more formal garden areas would be paradise for a growing child.

They had just finished exploring the extent of the grounds and from here, as they were exiting the yew-hedge-enclosed rose garden and joining a broad grass path that wound its way up to the house through double herbacious borders, Mytton Wells was revealed in all its eighteenth-century charm.

'Like our new house, Sophie?' He set his baby daughter down on her feet then straightened, draping an arm round Caro's slim shoulders. The casual intimacy seemed like the right, the only thing to do as he enquired softly, 'And what about you? What do you think of the place, Caro?'

Her opinion was important. She was important— crazy though that might seem in view of the short time he'd known her, and her seeming reluctance to trust him with the truth about herself.

'It's fantastic.' What else could she say? Mytton Wells *was* fantastic, as was the day, the time they'd spent excitedly exploring all the rooms together, poking their noses into every nook and cranny, exclaiming over the few bits and pieces of junk the previous inhabitants had left behind.

Fantastic. A fantasy. Something that couldn't be real or true. No matter how strong the feeling, there was nothing real about the feeling of joy and contentment, of coming home and belonging to each other, belonging to this place. Merely a fantasy.

And standing here with him, on this perfect, golden day, his body close, his arm around her as they watched the bright-haired child toddle along the wide grass path then sit down with a bump, her squeal of laughter like a silver bell, made tears spring scaldingly to her eyes because it was all a lie.

'Exactly.' The desire to haul her close against the length of his body and kiss her until they were both reeling, the ravenous hunger for her that clawed at him every time he saw her, touched her, or merely thought about her, was getting to be well-nigh un-manageable. He was going to have to do something about it, and soon.

He moved away from her, digging his hands deep into the pockets of his lightweight trousers. 'I'll fetch the things from the car; we might as well have our picnic here. And while I'm doing that I'll use the mo-bile to contact the owners of the place we were due to view this afternoon. Now we've seen Mytton Wells there's no point in looking at anything else.'

He'd been moving away from her, little by little, as he spoke, distancing himself physically because he found he couldn't trust himself when they were close. And Caro tore her eyes from him and fixed them on his child, now crawling across the path towards the flowery borders like a steam train.

'Fine. We'll find somewhere out of the sun. That big cedar at the side of the house, for instance?' She didn't wait for his reply, just scooped up Sophie and held the adorable scrap close to her heart and made her way to the end of the path, making a right-angle turn to take her to the side of the house, in the opposite direction to the one he was taking.

Unlike the house they'd been shown over yesterday and the one they had been due to inspect this afternoon, Mytton Wells was unoccupied. The estate agent had met them here this morning. Finn had accepted the keys, promised to return them later and suggested the agent leave them to it. Caro wished he hadn't.

The sensation of intimacy, the unreal feeling of belonging, had been growing all morning. Talk, laughter, exclamations over the views from the latticed windows, getting lost in the rambly attic rooms, discovering that their tastes in domestic architecture dovetailed perfectly—everything about the day so far had contrived to throw a golden, glowing veil over everything that was unpleasant. Unpleasant as in adulterer, deceiver, liar...

'Want down!' Sophie demanded, and Caro set the little girl on her feet and accepted the clasp of the tiny hand so trustingly held up to her. She knew she would miss this adorable child far more than she would ever have dreamed possible. Already she loved her and would deeply miss seeing her sunny smile each day.

Finn might be doing everything he could to give his daughter the ideal home, idyllic surroundings to grow up in, and he might love her devotedly, but she suspected that his relaxed attitude to his wedding vows had to be responsible for his wife's absence. He was effectively depriving his child of her mother for what he had admitted would be significant periods of time. Apart from those silver-framed photographs she might as well not exist.

The progress she and Sophie were making was so

slow, Finn caught up with them before they'd reached the shade-giving cedar. 'That's fixed.' He strode briefly ahead, tossing a rug down on the shaded grass. 'The estate agent will cancel this afternoon's appointment, and I've told him he'll be hearing from my solicitor regarding the sale of this place in the very near future. And we'll drop the keys off on our way back later this afternoon.'

He had flopped down on the soft green grass, was opening the cool-box. 'Get a move on, slowcoaches.' His eyes smiled up at them. 'I'm ravenous, so let's eat and enjoy the rest of the afternoon. And I'd like to take another look around inside before we make tracks.'

'Why?' Caroline settled Sophie down on the rug and sat beside her, her legs curled beneath her. 'You want to measure for curtains already?' She smiled at him, making a joke of it, keeping everything light because she knew she couldn't handle anything at all if things got heavy.

'No.' He grinned at her. 'I'll leave that sort of stuff to the experts. In the absence of a friendly, knowledgeable female I'll probably hire a firm of interior designers—but the job's yours, if you want it!'

Caro didn't rise to the bait. She took the buttered roll he handed her, broke it in half and handed a piece to Sophie. He had as good as told her that he and his wife lived more or less separate lives, that what he did had nothing to do with the absent Fleur, and she guessed he was going to use the rest of this lazy, lovely afternoon to try to coax his daughter's nanny into his bed!

And she wasn't being vain about that. No one could

mistake it. His body language, the way he looked at her, the gleam in the silvery eyes, the way his voice lowered, softened—everything about him spelled out his intentions.

Apart from the presence of the child who was now contentedly munching her way through a banana they were practically back to where they'd been last night.

The game was on again.

This time the build-up would be slower, of course, because Sophie was around, the fizzing sexual tension increasing because of that, and maybe this time he wouldn't give her the option of backing away.

Catching her breath, she wondered why she hadn't led him on last night, kept to her plan to get him really wound up, allowed the wretch to believe he'd scored yet again, then slapped him down at the very last moment.

The answer, she knew, was breathtakingly simple. As his eyes focused intensely on hers across the sweetly scented dappled shade, she knew that had things progressed any further, any further at all, she wouldn't have had the will-power to stop him from taking events to their natural conclusion, because when he touched her, or looked at her the way he was doing now, she turned into a mindless idiot.

A wanton, mindless idiot.

So it had to end now. The decision was sudden and completely certain. There would be no more games, no more half-crazed schemes to teach him what it felt like to be rejected. Cruelly rejected.

Before this afternoon was over she would tell him who she was, remind him of what he'd done to Katie, spell out the consequences of his thoughtless, heart-less treatment and leave.

The danger of taking the other path was far too great.

CHAPTER EIGHT

'NOT eating?' Finn, sitting on the grass with his long legs stretched out in front of him, leaned back on one elbow. The movement brought him slightly closer to his daughter's nanny.

The idle question elicited no response. The golden eyes were dark, troubled, the soft, lusciously pink lips parted, trembling just a little. Sublimely kissable lips...

'Aren't you hungry?'

'I...' She looked down at the buttered roll in one hand, the plump red tomato in the other and put them both down on the paper napkin he'd provided. 'No. I don't think I am.' Her voice sounded strained even to her own ears. She didn't know what she thought, what she wanted. She only knew that she wanted out of here, away from this man, out of this situation.

She turned away, agitatedly aware of the brevity of her shorts, the fully exposed length of leg, and wished she were wearing something smothering, preferably fashioned from mattress ticking because the rules of the game she'd been playing no longer applied.

'Something to drink, then?'

Without waiting for a reply he poured apple juice from a carton into a paper cup and gave it to her. She took it, taking enormous care to avoid touching his fingers, and sipped, watching with unwilling respect as he helped his tiny daughter drink from her beaker then gently settled the sleepy-eyed moppet down on the blanket, on her side, stroking the back of her starfish hands until the big brown eyes began to close.

'She's tired out—it's all the excitement and running around in the clean air. I'm glad Mytton Wells came on the market at the right time because I don't think I could ever have found anything else so perfect for us—she's going to love living here,' he said softly as he lifted his eyes from the now sleeping child. 'And you, Caro? How would you feel about living out here?'

It would be a wonderful place to live, but what did her opinion matter? She wouldn't be living here, even if she were given the option. Which she wouldn't be, not unless he was thinking of trying to persuade her to stay on as Sophie's permanent nanny. She had already told him she wouldn't consider doing that. So why should she bother to answer?

She shrugged his question away, slim shoulders lifting then falling indifferently, her mind already occupied with other things. Very soon now she was going to tell him how foul she thought he was, and tell him precisely why she thought that. The idea wasn't particularly appealing but she owed it to Katie.

'You prefer the city? Or is there a boyfriend in the background you'd miss?' Finn asked. The distinct possibility that there might be a man in her life hadn't seriously occurred to him before now. He couldn't imagine why it hadn't. He couldn't be the only man on the planet to find her irresistible. Unless, of course, he'd instinctively known she was his, or would be, the past presence of any other man in her life immaterial, not worth thinking about.

Suddenly his stomach felt as if it had tied itself up in knots. Painful knots. The thought of her in the arms of another man—any man—was torment.

'Well?' His voice was harsher than he'd intended, but, dammit, it looked as if she meant to ignore his question completely. And now he needed to know if there was another man in her life!

Another man? The use of those words implied that he, Finn Helliar, was already in her life. He wasn't, not yet. But he knew now that he fully intended to be.

The abrasion of his voice brought her head round. She'd been staring into the distance, her eyes fixed on the foaming green of the woodland trees, hardly daring to breathe because she was psyching herself up for what she had to do and say. For Katie's sake.

Conscious of the way he was looking at her, as if he needed and intended to get inside her head, she drew her knees up to her chin, wrapped both arms around them, glanced at him quickly then fixed her eyes on the peacefully sleeping baby.

She would answer his question; it was easy enough to do, and it would buy her a little more time before she said what she had to say and all hell broke loose.

'I don't think it's germane, but it's not a state secret, so no, I don't have preferences, not strong ones. City or countryside, I'm easy. As for boyfriends...' The look she gave him was consciously challenging. No need to smile, to gaze limpidly through lowered lashes, not any more. She was through trying to flirt with him. Leading him on in order to slap him back down no longer formed part of her game plan. 'There's no one in particular and nothing serious. An occasional theatre or dinner date; that's all I can make time for. I'm a career woman, first and foremost. And that doesn't mean I'm frigid,' she said challengingly.

'No?'

A dark brow quirked outrageously and she felt her face flame and, against her better judgement, found herself defending, 'Look—much as I love her, I can't help knowing my mother is the type of woman who can't stand on her own. She married young, and until Dad was killed in a riding accident she leaned on him, and after that she leaned on me, and, in a strange sort of way, on Gran. I don't want to be like that. I want to stand on my own, make a life of my own before I even think of sharing it with a man. So until I'm certain of who I am and where I'm going my career comes first.'

'Truly?' The glint in his eyes, the curve of his sexy mouth should have set warning bells ringing in her mind. He seemed to have moved closer, close enough for him to lift a hand, let his forefinger laze its slow, tormenting way down the length of her arm. His touch made her breath thicken and burn in her lungs. 'And what is your career? A life full of other people's babies—and none of your own?' His finger trailed its way back up her arm and when she opened her mouth to make an objection that same finger gently closed her lips, making her eyes go wide and dark with panic.

His own eyes gleamed with sudden satisfaction, his mouth practically curling with it, as if he could actually taste it on his tongue. 'You told me you never stayed with a family for more than a few weeks, otherwise you became too emotionally involved with your young charges.' He felt the soft quivering of her lush and lovely mouth beneath his finger and hated himself for teasing her, trying to drag the truth out of her, yet he continued softly, remorselessly, because one way or another he had to get her to admit the nanny deception. 'Doesn't that tell you anything?'

His finger wandered down to her chin and trailed slowly down the length of her throat, coming to rest in the small hollow at the base where he could feel the vital, wild thud of her pulses.

'Such as?' The counter-question was instinctive even though the words were physically difficult to form. This close, touching her, he seemed to have paralysed her, robbed her even of the will to move.

'Such as you need babies of your own.'

The thoughts that statement conjured up in his brain were definitely X-rated and, dammit, if she persisted in pretending to be a bona fide nanny then there was nothing he could do about it.

The need to take her in his arms again, to learn the shape of her—every last delightful curve and delicious hollow—both with his eyes and his hands, to take the taste of her into his mouth, was irresistible. He didn't think he was going to be able to wait until she decided she could trust him enough to tell him who she was and what she really did for a living.

And if he had read the signals right she was ready to respond to him. His hand moved to the nape of her neck and he saw her golden eyes haze with desire, her lips part softly under his gaze, and knew that should he ask her to stop him, as he had felt constrained to do last night, she would do nothing of the sort. Not this time.

But there was no hurry. It would be criminal to rush her, to force his way through to her by means of the purely physical. She had to be ready to respond to him emotionally, too.

They had all the time in the world, and besides, nothing earth-shattering could happen with his precious little daughter a mere few yards away. The fact that she was sound asleep made no difference at all.

However—his head dipped fractionally towards her, his hand cupping the back of her glossy head now—a kiss, just one, just a taste of her, the beginning of a slow, sweet build-up... A build-up that could last for days or even weeks but which would end, inevitably, in rapture.

He heard the tiny gasp she gave and sensed the sexual tension in her body, and—dear heaven!—how sweetly her breath fluttered against his mouth! The touch of her small hands as they crept up and splayed out against his ribcage was managing to send him out of his mind! And the way her full, rounded breasts brushed against his chest, the sensual contact scalding him through the thin cotton of his shirt, ignited flames that threatened to rage right out of control.

It was what had happened to her when he'd said she needed babies of her own that had done the mischief! Caro decided wildly. What he had said and the way he had said it in that slow, sexy voice of his that had started that primeval ache deep inside her, the sudden need for a baby of her own—for his baby...?

The way her thoughts were taking her made her panic. But not even panic could help her to move. It

paralysed her. It made her want to stay. Here. Right
here. With him. She didn't know what was happening,
only that they were both highly aroused, incapable of
stopping what was happening to them.

One of his hands was behind her head and his lips
were a breath away from hers. She took a gulp of air,
feeling the tight flowering of her breasts, the way they
pushed against him as if drawn, body to body, mouth
to mouth... Her hands clutched at him, holding him,
the heat and hardness of his body making her head
spin, and she saw his eyes glitter hotly, darkly, just a
split second before his mouth curved with a heart-
jolting sensuality and moved swiftly to cover her own.

Her own lips met his, responding, slow, erotic
strokes and softly moist explorations turning to wild,
unthinking demands as together they sank back on the
grass, feverish bodies entwined as he lifted his mouth
from hers, pushing her tumbled hair back from her
face with a slightly unsteady hand, holding her eyes
with the intensity of his as if to reinforce and give
credence to his hoarsely uttered words. 'Caro, I can't
help it if you think I'm crazy—but, hell, I think I'm
falling in love with you!'

His words acted like a bucket of icy water, bringing
her cruelly to her senses. He didn't know the meaning
of the word; men like him used lies like that to talk
gullible women into their beds all the time. And, even
if the world was pear-shaped and he was telling the
truth, he wasn't free to do any such thing!

How could she have given in to the wicked
thoughts and desires that he alone seemed capable of
creating, responded so lustily to such a man?

Shame made it almost impossible to speak, definitely impossible to bunch up her fists and push him away. And when she could get her words out they were instinctive. The means to hurt him, to take the revenge that had been handed to her on a plate. And the words emerged huskily on the merest thread of sound. 'I wonder what your wife would think if she heard you saying that?'

Muzzily, she realised that earlier she had given up on the idea of making him bite the bullet of sexual frustration as a way of exacting a measure of revenge for what he had done to Katie. But the situation had somehow presented itself and the words had come out of her mouth as if they'd been programmed to do so, and the effect that the reminder of his wife had had on him was everything she could have hoped for.

He went very still, every muscle and sinew taut and strained, and she saw the colour drain from his face, his eyes go black with some bleak emotion before he gathered himself and pushed away from her, swung round, his back to her as he pushed his fingers roughly through his thick dark hair.

Finn got to his feet, his face harsh, mirroring his thoughts.

He could barely believe he'd heard that. The first woman to make him feel like a lovesick adolescent at the mercy of his hormones for God only knew how many years, the first woman ever to arouse a whole raft of masculine protectiveness he had never known he possessed, the desire to cherish and respect as well as the desire to bed. All these crazy emotions shown up for the folly that they were by those husky, taunting words of hers.

He had believed himself in love for the first time

in his life. In love with a woman who would have had sex with a man she believed to be married.

Her partner back at the agency had obviously omitted to pass on the information that the Mrs Helliar who had accompanied him from Canada, who was presently visiting with friends in the London area, was his mother. She had responded to every advance he had made, initiating a few of her own, all the time believing him to be a married man.

He was blisteringly angry with them both. With himself for putting her on a pedestal, with her for having feet of clay right up to her pretty neck!

CHAPTER NINE

'FLEUR—my wife—died before Sophie was a month old.' His words dropped heavily, coldly, and when he turned to face her again his features displayed no expression at all. Except, perhaps, distaste.

Soft-footed, he moved to where his daughter slept in the dappled shade of the tree, dark lashes fanning her flushed chubby cheeks. Finn picked the little girl up and cradled her carefully in his arms, his lips barely moving as he instructed tersely, 'Pack everything up, will you? We're leaving. I'll wait for you at the car.'

Caro watched him walk away. She felt physically sick, her heart jumping about dementedly under her ribs. The warm, still summer afternoon was suddenly oppressive. Yet she shuddered.

His wife was dead. The knowledge stunned her. All the time she'd been in his employ she'd almost been inventing him to fit into the shoes of the character she'd believed him to be: a philanderer whose lack of loving commitment had driven his wife back to her abandoned career, the type of man who would play around with his personal secretary, not to mention his daughter's nanny, while his wife was out of sight.

But he didn't have a wife. Fleur Helliar had been dead for over a year.

Caro knew she'd done him an enormous injustice and she felt truly bad about that. But, in her own defence, no one, least of all Finn, had explained the situation to her. And who the heck had the sultry Sandra been talking about when she'd mentioned Mrs Helliar?

Gloomily, she re-packed the picnic things and folded the blanket and followed to where he'd parked the car. Her mention of his wife had obviously done something to put him off the idea of going over the house he wanted to buy again this afternoon. She knew he'd been looking forward to doing just that but now he couldn't wait to get away. She felt bad about that, too.

Had he loved Fleur so very much? Could the mere mention of her name, even after this length of time, still affect him so deeply?

The bleak look he gave her as he took the baggage from her to stow in the back of the off-roader told her she must have hit on the truth and she whispered impulsively, 'Finn, I'm sorry!'

Despite the hurt he had dished out to Katie, she really meant it; she was sorry. Sorry to have misjudged him to such an extent, sorry to have given him pain by forcing him to mention the tragic loss of his wife at such an early age.

The depth of her regret both puzzled and worried her. As did his curt, 'As soon as we've cleared up at the cottage we'll head back to London.' He had already strapped the still sleeping Sophie into her car seat and was holding the passenger-side door open, waiting with barely concealed impatience for her to clamber up.

She shot a perplexed look into his stony face, learned absolutely nothing, so shrugged, just slightly, and climbed up into her seat and stared blankly out of the windscreen until he swung up into the driver's seat and turned the key in the ignition.

He didn't give what would hopefully be his future home the merest flicker of a glance as he swung the chunky vehicle in a half circle then headed off down the drive, and Caro, deciding to give it one more shot, said, 'I hadn't realised you were a single parent—I wasn't told that was your reason for wanting a nanny for Sophie. I wouldn't have mentioned your wife the way I did—' To her dismay she felt her face go pink. 'I had no idea she was dead.'

'So I gather.' His tone was dry, cutting. 'However, on consideration, this single parent can cope. As of this evening—when we get back to the hotel—your employment is terminated. You can scurry back to your agency and get down to the paperwork, or whatever it is you normally do when wearing your director's hat. Though, if you're as bad at that as you are at knowing one end of a baby from another, then the ignominious and early demise of the Grandes Familles Agency would come as no surprise whatsoever.'

Caro's eyes went wide. 'So you knew,' she muttered as soon as she could gather sufficient breath to speak.

'Of course.'

'And you said nothing?' There she'd been, merrily plotting her plots and scheming her schemes, stupidly thinking he didn't know her from Adam and would never connect her with Katie—oh, what a fool that made her feel!

'I was waiting for you to tell me why you were

his silver eyes turn black and hard, his mouth turn down in angry, bitter contempt.

He reached for his mobile phone and said pointedly, 'Lost the use of your legs? If not, I'd like to make a private call.'

'Oh—go jump off a cliff!' Caro scrambled out of the car and headed up the garden path. That explosion of temper, childish as it undeniably was, actually helped. Helped a lot. It pushed all those tearful, wimpish notions of actually caring about the wretched man, finding him sexy as hell, and about as resistible as chilled spring water on a scorching summer day, right into limbo where they belonged. And replaced the whole bunch of idiotic illusions with good old-fashioned rage!

It took no time at all to throw her things into a bag and strip her bed and Sophie's cot. She had no idea what the loathsome Finn intended to do about the laundry and as sure as hens laid eggs she wasn't going to ask!

But stuffing Horn into the canvas hold-all with the rest of the baby's things brought the tears flooding back, filling her eyes and making her feel a fool.

Despite the golden-haired charmer being the dreaded Finn's offspring, fruit of his loins, as it were, she would miss the little girl dreadfully. Sophie had burrowed her way into her incompetent nanny's heart in rather less time than it took to blink.

Grumbling at herself for allowing an emotion that wasn't anger anywhere near her, Caro dumped the packed bags in the tiny hallway for Finn to find or fall over—she didn't care which—and went outside to sit on the garden wall and wait until he'd finished doing whatever it was he was doing and was ready to leave.

The journey back into London was a nightmare. Bored and hot, Sophie started to grizzle. Caro did her best to amuse her, but with scant success. Finn kept a tight-lipped silence. The traffic as they neared the capital was horrendous and the afternoon got hotter and increasingly airless.

A deep longing to be back in the open countryside again, breathing the sweet, clean air and listening to the silence, assailed her as she stood on the dusty pavement outside Finn's hotel with the ever-present roar of the traffic annoying her ears.

Sighing, she shifted Sophie in her arms and tenderly brushed the tendrils of soft pale hair back from her hot little forehead. She'd give anything if only she could put the clock back, back to the time when Finn was holding her, telling her he thought he was falling in love with her.

Anything at all.

That particular piece of knowledge didn't bring her much joy. How could it when it meant she was in danger of doing the unthinkable—falling in love with him? She was free to do that now—now she knew he was a single man. The only thing that had stopped her admitting the possibility before had been her belief that there was a wife somewhere in the background.

But, in any case, the devious louse had been telling lies when he'd talked about falling in love. She knew that, didn't she?

'Righto, Soph!' She made herself smile, made herself swallow the stupid great lump in her throat. 'Why don't I take you up and pop you in the bath to cool off? Does that sound good to you?'

Finn had given her the key to the suite of rooms, ordered her to take his daughter up, told her to wait quietly until he joined them in a couple of minutes, and zoomed away to park the car in the hotel's underground car park. She poked a finger into the little fat tummy and tickled up a gale of squeals and gurgles which made a lovely change from grizzles and lasted all the way up to the suite.

She wouldn't think about how much she would miss both the man and his child; she would concentrate on getting her life back again. Nice and safe and sane. No Finn around to mess up her head, wreak havoc with her hormones, no puzzles to make her doubt her own sanity—and his.

But before she left she would tell him why she had applied for the job in the first place, explain everything, about Katie and what his treatment of her had done to her. It would be more in sorrow than in anger, not the bitter castigation she had originally meant to lash him with.

Apart from his being the most gorgeous, the sexiest, most charismatic male she had ever encountered, or was ever likely to encounter, he had something else that drew her even more strongly. A basic kindness, a warmth, a lack of that arrogant male superiority that in many other successful men had made her hackles rise, made her secretly despise them.

Except for his unfathomable reaction to hearing her talk about his dead wife and the reprehensible masculine trait of telling a girl what he thought she wanted to hear, Finn Helliar had now come to seem pretty well perfect.

It was difficult to imagine him knowingly hurting anyone. Maybe he hadn't realised how very much in love with him Katie had been. Or maybe—and this was the more likely supposition—Katie herself had blown everything up out of all proportion. She had always tended to over-dramatise herself.

As she opened the door to Finn's suite of rooms the telephone began to ring and, anchoring Sophie to her knee with one hand, she sat on a sofa to answer it.

'Gran?' Winged brows drew together over golden eyes. 'Is anything wrong?'

'Of course there is! Why else should I be phoning? I've been trying to get you since midday. That woman who works for you gave me Helliar's number, though why— Oh, never mind that now. You have to come immediately. Your mother had an accident; her car's a write-off and she's in Intensive Care. Stanning General—the prognosis is not at all good. You need to come at once.'

Caro tried to speak but couldn't. She wanted to tell her grandmother she'd be there as soon as she possibly could but couldn't get the words out. There was an unbearable tightness in her chest and the room was swaying, misty and dark, and Finn walked through the mist, closing the door behind him.

'Caroline? Are you still there?'

Her grandmother's imperious tone helped her to pull herself together and she answered thinly, 'I'll be with you as soon as I can.' She frowned up at Finn as he took the baby from her, hovering over her, his dark brows peaked in query.

'Good. And is young Helliar there? If so, I need to speak to him, too.'

She couldn't imagine why and felt too numb to ask, simply handed the receiver over and stood up, rubbing her temples with the tips of her fingers, wondering whether it would be quicker to phone for a cab or make the time to go and collect her own car.

Finn put the receiver down a few moments later and Caro turned and held her hand out.

'May I call a cab? I need one to take me to the hospital. When I've seen Mum I'll arrange to collect my own car.'

'In a moment.' He put Sophie on the floor and stood up, his concerned eyes raking her pale face. 'Five minutes, that's all. There are a couple of calls I have to make and then I'll see you get to the hospital.'

How selfish could a man get? 'I don't believe this!'

'Trust me.' He began to punch numbers and Caro, grinding her teeth, turned away. Revising her former opinion of his 'kindness and warmth', she collected Sophie and Horn and took them both to the bedroom. At least she could use the time to freshen up and change into something more suitable for a sickbed vigil. She wondered if Katie was coping, if she was sitting at their mother's bedside or if she'd taken fright, hiding herself in a corner back at home, crying her eyes out.

Fuming at the unnecessary delay forced on her by that inconsiderate beast, Caro sluiced her hands and face with cold water, changed her shorts and T-shirt for a wrap-around cotton skirt and sleeveless blouse and dragged a comb through her hair.

She should be there, at the hospital, sitting with her mum, giving Katie the support she would need, allowing her sister to lean on her strength. It wasn't that Katie was mentally feeble—she was insecure, unsure of herself; she needed constant reassurances.

That was why she should be on her way to her right now, not waiting while Finn concluded his vital phone calls—probably to his solicitor about getting the ball rolling towards the purchase of Mytton Wells, and to the sultry Sandra, telling her to get herself over here to keep him company.

It would only have taken her one minute, if that, to phone for a cab—

'Everything's going to be fine—'

'Why the hell can't you learn to knock?' she spat out at him, goaded beyond endurance. He'd forced her to delay that call for a cab, was mouthing meaningless platitudes about everything being all right—of all the facile... And yet, dammit all, her heart soared and swelled at the sight of him and she wanted him to take her in his arms and comfort her. She wanted to lean on someone for a change, instead of being leant upon.

Not any old someone. Only him.

'Caro—it's OK, I promise.' The reassurance of his voice and his smile would have soothed an elephant with tusk-ache. Her eyes glimmered at him suspiciously between dark and tangled lashes. 'I phoned the hospital to get the facts straight,' he told her. 'Elinor had more or less said that there was little or no hope for your mother's recovery and because I imagine she said the same thing to you I needed to check.'

He searched her face with narrowed eyes. 'The accident happened early this morning. She had been unconscious ever since, but is now awake and doing fine—apart from cracked ribs, an acre or so of bruising, and the remnants of concussion. She's already out of Intensive Care and in a side ward— Hey—'

His arms steadied her as she swayed on her feet, relief weakening her. He half carried her into the sitting room and led her to the sofa. 'It's not a life and death situation, I promise you, so relax for half an hour. My mother will be with us by then—that was the second call I had to make. She'll stay here with Sophie and I'll drive you to the hospital.'

Tears washed her eyes and spangled her lashes. Again she had misjudged him. Horribly. He had taken charge, sorted everything out, made everything so very much better.

She gave him a wobbly smile. 'I should have questioned everything Gran said myself instead of leaping at a tangent. I know her a lot better than you do and should have remembered how she unfailingly dramatises each and every situation.'

A tendency Katie had inherited, but whereas the old lady dramatised for effect and to make herself appear even tougher than she undoubtedly was Katie created dramas so that she could lie down under them and wail!

'And you really don't have to drive me. I am capable of sitting in the back of a cab—I know you say Mum's going to be fine—and I'm grateful to you for finding out—' She got to her feet, annoyed to find herself swaying, not knowing why she was feeling so light-headed, doing her best to make her voice sound firm as she told him, 'I could be on my way now, not sitting here—'

'Stay where you are.' The lightest pressure from his hands on her shoulders eased her back amongst the cushions. 'Your grandmother appeared to be in quite a state. I think your mother's accident brought home the fact of her own mortality. She wants advice on all those trust funds—my father helped set them up, remember? He and your grandfather were old friends.' He stood back, hands on hips, watching her closely as if to satisfy himself she wasn't about to pop back to her feet like a jack-in-the-box. 'So I might as well kill two birds with one stone—get to the bottom of what she wants to do about the trusts and deliver you to the hospital. You've had a shock, don't forget, so do yourself a favour and relax. I'll get Room Service to bring up some tea.'

Satisfied she was staying put, he used the phone to order up Sophie's milk and Caroline's tea. A frowning glance at his watch told him his mother should arrive in less than an hour. Until then he would have to keep a firm grip on his tongue and a firmer one on his emotions.

On the way back from the cottage he had been practically counting the minutes until she would be right out of his life. He had been on the point of making a fool of himself, had actually believed he'd fallen in love with the minx.

How could his judgement have been so way off the mark? How could he have imagined himself in love with the type of woman who would fall into the arms of a married man—at least a man she fully believed to be married, with a young child into the bargain? Not only fall into his arms but respond to his kisses, revel in his caresses, and give every impression of being ready for very much more!

He felt as if he'd been slapped in the face. He felt hurt and betrayed. Yes, dammit, he felt as if she'd betrayed him, as if she'd offered him something indescribably beautiful only to let him discover that the glittering shell covered something vile and loathsome.

Yet no way could he let her cope with the trauma of her mother's accident on her own. From what he could remember of her sister Katie she would be more of a liability than a help in this sort of situation.

Besides, he had to see old Elinor Farr at some time in the very near future. He could get that over with and deliver Caroline to her mother's bedside on the same journey. Do what was right then wash the whole troublesome family out of his hair.

Caro rubbed her fingers over her forehead. Everything was in a muddle. His mother had to be the Mrs Helliar Sandra had spoken of. And when she herself had spoken of his needing Mrs Helliar's opinion before he went ahead and purchased a new house she had been referring to his wife and he, of course, had been talking of his mother when he'd said she would be in England only one month out of twelve.

'So your mother doesn't live here,' Caro said, wondering why he looked so tense. Something was bugging him and she didn't know what it was and it was doing her head in.

If she was going to have to spend more time with

him then she supposed she must try to keep everything normal on the surface. Forget he'd sacked her,
acted as if he loathed her—for absolutely no good
reason that she could see—then turned into something
her mother would have called A Tower Of Strength,
in capital letters. Forget that she only had to look at
him to grow weak with longing.

'No.' Something caught at his throat and filled it,
tugged at his heart and nearly broke it. At least, that
was what it felt like, he amended savagely. Sophie,
tired of crawling round the furniture, had clambered
up on Caroline's lap, wound her chubby arms around
her nanny's neck, and tucked her curly head into the
curve of that same nanny's elegant neck.

They made the perfect picture. He couldn't drag his
eyes away. And it hadn't been so very long ago that
he'd had the desire to see her hold their baby in her
arms, love her until the end of his days, care for her
and their children, provide and protect. His thoughts
were becoming intolerable.

He cleared the tightness from his throat, called
'Come!' as a room-service waiter tapped on the door,
and answered Caroline's question. 'Lucy, my mother,
settled back in her native Canada after my father died.
Up until then they'd been enjoying Dad's retirement
in the south of France. Tea?'

He handed her a steaming cup, whether she wanted
it or not, and sat Sophie back against the cushions
with her feeding beaker of milk. 'She came over with
us for a holiday. She's visiting with friends in Surrey
but she's more than happy to come and baby-mind
Sophie for a couple of days while I get to grips with

whatever it is that's rattling your formidable grandmother.'

He watched her assimilate the information he'd given her while she took small, not very interested sips of tea. Elinor Farr had called her eldest granddaughter a chip off the old block. But was that true? Staunch, intelligent, strong and forceful—yes, he'd go along with that. But one thing was out of kilter. Elinor Farr wasn't sneaky and devious, lacking in moral fibre. Caroline Farr, as he'd discovered, was.

Over the next few hours, stuck with her as he was, he would do well to remember that.

CHAPTER TEN

FINN was bathing the baby when Lucy Helliar arrived.

'Sophie's had a very busy day,' Caro explained. 'So Finn thought it best to get her to bed before we left because if she knew you were here she'd get over-excited and wouldn't sleep.'

'Oh, bless her!' Lucy flopped down on the sofa and patted her iron-grey curls into place. 'He's quite right, of course. I've missed the little treasure. I helped Finn bring her up, you know, right from the first. Poor Fleur was too ill—is that fresh tea in the pot?'

'No, but I'll ring down for some.'

'Oh, don't go to that trouble.' She reached for one of the tiny cucumber sandwiches left untouched from the tea that had been served earlier. 'Fix me up a gin and tonic from the mini bar, there's a good girl, and tell me how you like working for that son of mine. I was truly pleased when he let me know he'd got fixed up with a nanny for Sophie so soon. He's very good with her but he's not going to be able to be with her twenty-four hours a day for ever, is he? And do give me your honest opinion of that property he's thinking of buying. He phoned, earlier this afternoon, and told me the news—that he'd found the house he wanted to buy.'

Lucy Helliar was so open and friendly, she practically took Caro's breath away. She only wished the lady's son had inherited some of that openness, then she wouldn't have to keep tormenting her mind wondering why he was acting the way he was.

He had obviously phoned his mother on the mobile outside the borrowed cottage when he'd rudely asked her if she'd lost the use of her legs, emphasising his need for privacy. He might have told his mum about Mytton Wells but he obviously hadn't told her he'd already sacked the new nanny. And Caro wasn't about to remedy the omission.

'I think you'll love the house when you see it.' She set the drink on the low table in front of the sofa. 'I know your son thinks it will be the perfect place for little Sophie to grow up in. Perhaps you'll love it so much you'll consider making your home there with them?'

Perhaps she shouldn't have said that—she was fully aware that it really wasn't any of her business—but she suddenly ached to hear that Finn's little girl would have her grandmother around when her father was, of necessity, away working. She didn't like to think of the tiny girl being brought up by professional carers.

'No, I shan't be living in England. Oh, I'm not saying I won't visit—of course I will. For a couple of months at a time each year. You might call me selfish, but I have my own life, home, family and friends back in my own country. And Finn and Sophie have their life here. It was Finn's wish and choice to return to the land of his birth and make a home for them both. Of course, it was only natural that he should bring Fleur to me after their marriage. We knew by then that she was so dreadfully ill.'

Lucy patted the sofa. 'Please sit down while you're waiting for Finn. And tell me all about yourself.'

Again the friendly invitation, but Caro couldn't do that. She really, really couldn't.

How could she possibly tell this nice friendly soul that she was no more a nanny than her next-door neighbour's cat was, that she had sneaked her way in here with the express intention of seeking revenge? And she wasn't going to tell any more lies. Which left, 'I'd rather you told me about little Sophie's mother.'

For some reason she couldn't bring herself to refer to Fleur as having been Finn's wife and the aversion had nothing whatsoever to do with her protective feelings for her sister.

It had more to do with the way she was beginning to feel about him: as if she couldn't bear to let him out of her sight, as if he belonged to her and no one else. And if she knew more about the glamorous French singer, Fleur Ferrand, and what had happened to her, then she might feel closer to him. She wanted to know everything about every part of his life.

'So Finn didn't give you the details.' Lucy sipped her drink reflectively, then set the glass down, nodding slowly. 'He doesn't like to discuss it, and that's perfectly understandable when one considers the circumstances. Such a terrible tragedy.'

Her eyes lingered on one of the silver-framed photographs. 'She was so lovely, wasn't she? Finn insists those photographs are on display wherever they happen to be so that Sophie will always know who her mother was and what she looked like. And apparently she'd suddenly shot to fame and had a great future ahead of her in the pop music world.'

She sighed deeply, shaking her head. 'Fleur would

have hated to think that what happened to her became public knowledge. She always said she wanted the public, especially back in her native France, to remember her as being young, beautiful and successful. But as Sophie's nanny I guess you have a right to know. At least, you should know about the illness that claimed her life.'

'Not if it's personal—private—' Caro floundered. She felt perfectly dreadful. A low-life of the sneakiest possible kind. She had no right to know anything.

And how easily Lucy had been deflected from her request to learn more about her granddaughter's nanny; how generously had the elderly lady offered to give her details on a private family tragedy. She was going to have to confess, tell Lucy Helliar that she was no longer in her son's employ—

'She's out for the count.' Finn walked through, buttoning the cuffs of the crisp white shirt he'd changed into as he came to greet his parent with a hug. 'Thanks for coming. I wouldn't have asked you to break into your visit if it hadn't been important. I should be back later tonight, but if I think I need to stay longer with Elinor Farr I'll let you know. Dad helped set up some complicated trust funds when her husband, Ambrose, was alive, remember?'

'Very well,' Lucy concurred. 'They were great friends. And you must stay as long as you feel you need to.'

'Just long enough to find out why she suddenly feels there's cause for anxiety.' He shot a look at his wristwatch, his voice cooling noticeably as he asked, 'Ready, Caroline?'

She nodded, her throat closing up. He was looking

at her as if she were a particularly virulent form of poison. She collected her shoulder bag and the canvas hold-all she'd packed the rest of her gear into and Lucy said, 'I do hope your mother makes a full and rapid recovery. But don't worry about this end—I'm more than happy to take your place for as long as you need. I've got plenty of time to go visit my friends again.'

'So you didn't explain that I'd thrown you off the job,' Finn remarked coldly a few minutes later as the lift carried them down to street level. 'You let her think you'd be coming right back. What a devious, sneaky little creature you are.'

He knew his reaction was over the top. It was perfectly understandable that she would have felt embarrassed at having to explain.

But he wanted to lash out at her and grabbed any excuse to do so because he couldn't give her the real reason for his bitter anger. He couldn't admit to her that he felt angry enough to shake her until her teeth dropped out because he'd come within a whisker of falling in love with her. And while he didn't expect her to be an angel he didn't want her to be the type of woman who'd play around with a married man.

Caro gave him a cold look, sick of his evil temper, and yes, OK, she really should have explained the situation to Lucy, and she felt bad about prying into what had happened to his dead wife. But she hadn't learned anything and he wasn't so all-fired perfect, was he?

'You should be thankful I kept my mouth shut.' She glared at him, no longer afraid to meet his eyes because of the contempt that was there every time he looked at her now. 'If I'd told your mother you'd sacked me because I'm not the qualified nanny I pretended to be—and I'm not so sure about that,' she added witheringly, 'since you claim you knew I wasn't all along and were apparently perfectly happy to say nothing at all about it—then I would have had to tell her why I stooped to such devious behaviour to get the job in the first place.'

She walked out, her head high, as the lift doors whooshed open and he didn't say a word until they were both in the car, which had been brought round for him and was waiting on double yellow lines. And then he asked, his voice as smooth and cold as a steel blade, 'And why exactly did you stoop to what you've admitted was devious behaviour? To earn a few extra bucks to plough back into an ailing business? Or did you have a darker motive? I think I'm beginning to know you well enough to suspect the latter.'

He put the engine into gear and edged out into the early evening traffic and Caro wished she'd insisted on hiring a cab to take her to the hospital. But she hadn't and he'd asked a question and she was going to give him the answer and he didn't have to like it.

'I wanted to hurt you for what you did to my sister Katie. Remember her? Katie Farr? I thought a great opportunity would present itself if I worked for you.' She risked a look at his profile. Clear-cut, unforgiving, the sensual mouth compressed. She transferred her gaze back to the rear end of the red London bus they were stuck behind. 'Not one of my better ideas, as it happens.'

'And your grandmother always claimed you were so level-headed. Did you know,' he tossed out conversationally, 'the way she talked about you, you could well have been some kind of sainted super-woman? A right pain in the you-know-what. With respect, she's such an opinionated old lady, learning just how wrong she is about you could seriously damage her health. So shall we make a pact not to tell her?'

'Whereas your halo shines in the dark,' Caro came back, almost light-headedly, 'for all to see and wonder at.' It made her feel giddy, the way they were calling each other names, but oh, so very politely. She gripped her hands into fists, making her fingernails bite into the tender skin of her palms, primarily to stop herself from bursting into hysterical laughter.

It wasn't funny.

'Yet at the moment you appear to believe it's tarnished.' He saw the traffic snarl-up ahead and made an avoiding left turn into a side street. 'Would you like to explain exactly what it is I did to Katie? But tell me, did she ever get around to doing something about that floral decorator's business she was so keen to set up?'

'I don't know what you're talking about.'

'No? Then Katie doesn't confide in you? I wonder why? Too much in awe of her brilliant big sister?'

'Hardly.' Remembering how Katie had always run to her with her problems, big or little—and mostly little—real or imaginary—and mostly always imaginary until Finn had entered her life and turned it sour—Caro sighed and Finn took his eyes off the now relatively quiet road ahead to shoot her a sardonic look.

'Hit a nerve? Does that mournful sigh mean a smidgen of contrition?'

'It means you're talking through the back of your head. I don't know whether you make a habit of it, but in this case I'm finding it a bit tedious. Get your facts straight, Finn.'

'And they are?'

He didn't sound so laid-back now. There was a very slight edge to his voice.

Caro gave him a quick appraising glance, found his profile an enigma as usual and let him have it in a voice as cool and impersonal as she could make it. 'Katie confides in me. Not in Gran—she's terrified of her. Not in Mum, either, because she tends to get in a flap. But she tells me things. Such as why she tried to drown herself.'

She heard the harsh, disbelieving inward drag of his breath and ignored it, reminding him, 'She was head over heels in love with you and believed you loved her. Do you always tell them you think you're falling in love? Have you found it the quickest way to get them into bed? It certainly worked with Katie, didn't it?'

Aware of the sudden brittleness that had appeared in her voice, of the interpretation he just might put on the reason for it, she smoothed down the sharp edges and swooped for the jugular. 'She could see no reason for living when she woke up one morning and saw your wedding photographs splashed all over the front of her newspaper. The fact that your bride was well and truly pregnant with your child didn't help much, either. I wanted to hurt you back. For her.'

His silence alarmed her; it made the hairs on the back of her neck stand up on end. If he told her that it was all lies, that he barely knew Katie and certainly hadn't seduced her, she knew, to her eternal shame, she would believe him because she didn't want to believe he was that bad.

Much as she loved her younger sister, she had to admit that Katie had always had a penchant for self-dramatisation, a sometimes worrying habit of appearing to shut herself away in a dream world of her own making.

Believing him would free her up to admit her true feelings for him. She didn't want to do that, didn't want to fall in love with a man who really and truly disliked her because she had mentioned his still deeply mourned dead wife and sullied her memory by daring to speak of her.

The blistering silence continued and of course he could have been concentrating on his driving, but they were well on the open road now and the traffic was relatively light, so it looked as though he was trying to come to terms with what she'd told him, perhaps trying to dream up excuses and come up smelling of roses.

But she knew he couldn't even be bothered to do that when he said, 'We're about ten minutes away from the hospital. We're going to have to talk about what you've told me. But not right now.'

CHAPTER ELEVEN

'Too silly.' Emma Farr's eyes drifted shut at last, her lashes dark, fluttering smudges against her white skin. 'Daydreaming.'

Daydreaming and didn't see the other car rounding the bend in the narrow lane, her instinctive evasive action heading her straight into a high stone wall, according to the information Katie had given her.

'Don't try to talk, Mum. That's good; rest as much as you can,' Caro approved softly.

Katie looked at her sister with big, big eyes and whispered, 'It's great to see her sleeping naturally. Before, it was awful; we thought she'd never regain consciousness.'

Emma Farr, given time, was going to be fine, so the young doctor in charge of her case had affirmed. After getting this expert prognosis Finn had delivered her to the door of Emma's private room and had left without a word, not even saying goodbye, striding away as fast as his long legs would carry him.

And goodbye to you, too, Caro had muttered darkly inside her head, swallowing tears and anger in equal measure. So much for his suggestion that they discuss Katie's accusations at a more convenient time. If he'd had any intention of doing that he would have made some mention of it, told her he'd be in touch.

He'd done nothing of the sort. Simply made himself

129

scarce. If she ever heard from him again she'd turn into a monkey's uncle!

Which meant he had to be the louse she'd believed him to be right at the start, before his charisma and her suddenly over-active hormones had made her doubt.

'Maybe we should leave now she's asleep?' she suggested, noting Katie's pallor, the droop of her shoulders.

She felt deeply ashamed of herself. How could she have allowed that creep to influence her to the extent of being on the point of believing he could do no wrong, and that Katie, her own dearly loved kid sister, had made the whole thing up?

'You've had a long and worrying day. And there's nothing either of us can do here now. Sleep is the best medicine Mum can get at the moment and we'll come in again in the morning.'

Tears stung her eyes. Her mother looked so small and frail hooked up to that drip. But she was going to be all right, and that was what counted.

'Did Gran make it to the hospital?' she asked as they tiptoed quietly from the room, and Katie shook her head.

'No. I don't think she felt she could face it. You know—the journey, the waiting around. David was here with me for most of the time—until Mum regained consciousness, that is. Otherwise I don't think I could have faced it, either. Not on my own. He went back when we knew Mum was going to be OK—he's got his dogs to feed and let out for a run. He kept Gran informed by phone, and she phoned you. Have you got your car?'

Caro shook her head. David Parker, her grandmother's head gardener, certainly had a happy knack of coming to the rescue, she thought approvingly, her mouth twitching when Katie went decidedly pink and offered, 'You can come back with us, then.' She looked at her watch. 'Dave said he'd come and collect me at eight. It's nearly that now. We'll wait in the car park, shall we?'

'That young man deserves a rise,' Caro said drily as they walked out of the hospital together. 'You should learn to drive, Katie.'

'I know. Dave's promised to teach me.'

'You get on well with him.'

'Very.' Katie bit her lip. 'I—I work with him in the gardens now. Old George finally retired and I suggested I took his place; I've always loved plants and flowers, you know that.'

Caro stood back for Katie to precede her through the door to the visitors' car park, her golden eyes thoughtful. Finn had mentioned something about a floral decorator's business, hadn't he? She let it go. For now.

'Don't tell me Gran pays you a wage?'

'She does so!' Katie grinned. 'She refused to think of my working in the gardens at first. Said I was just playing around. But Dave insisted, and not even Gran dares to go against him—she relies on him for much more than keeping the grounds beautiful now that the Fairchilds are getting so long in the tooth.

'So she pays me what she's graciously pleased to call ''apprenticeship wages''—just means roughly half of what Old George was getting—just to let everyone know she still calls the shots! Oh, look.' She had been scanning the arrivals and now her face lit up. 'There he is!'

Dave Parker drove an elderly Volvo estate and he was just as attractive and reliable-looking as ever. And Caro breathed a silent sigh of relief as his eyes lit up when he saw Katie waiting.

At least whatever her sister obviously felt for her grandmother's gardener wasn't one-sided, a fact confirmed by events when, half an hour later, he dropped them off at the lodge.

Caro, dumping her bags in the porch and turning, waiting for Katie who had the doorkey, noted the lingering lover-like kiss with satisfaction.

'It's serious, is it?' she asked when a few minutes later the Volvo's tail-lights disappeared down the lane.

'We plan to marry in the autumn,' Katie confided. 'Gran might not like it, but she'll have to lump it. You know what she's like, the rage she'll get into when she hears a member of the exalted Farr family is actually going to marry a servant!

'Do you think one of us should go over and see if she's all right? I know she has the Fairchilds and Polly to dance attendance and bow to her every whim but you know how miffed she gets if she thinks one of us is neglecting her.'

'I'll phone through and let her know we're back from the hospital later,' Caro offered. She needed to talk to her sister. They had gravitated to the kitchen, flicking lights on as they went. Caro gave silent thanks to the absent Dave because his relationship with her sister appeared to have given her the confidence to stand up for herself for the first time in her life. She could actually talk about the possibility of displeasing her grandmother without going pale and shaking in her shoes.

However, there was something she had to know, something that might shake all that new-found confidence. 'As far as I know, Finn Helliar's still up at the big house with Gran.'

'Finn? Helliar? Why should he be here?'

Katie's face had gone scarlet. 'Something to do with those trust funds,' Caro said, and picked up the kettle. 'Tea?'

'No.' Katie sat down heavily at the kitchen table. 'There's an opened bottle of wine in the fridge. Let's have that, shall we?'

'Why not?' As Caro found glasses and poured out the chilled Spätlese she pondered on the best approach to use. Reminding her sister, now happily looking forward to marriage with David Parker, that two years ago she had tried to kill herself for love of Finn Helliar was a bit of a facer. The wine might help smooth over a few awkward moments.

She wouldn't have mentioned Finn's name but she needed to know Katie was well and truly over him, not still pining in the secret places of her heart for the man she had loved and lost. Only then could she herself begin the process of forgetting him and the strangely ambiguous relationship they had.

'How did you know he was up at the house with Gran?' Katie asked in a careful little voice. 'You don't know him, do you?'

'I've had dealings with him through the agency,' Caro answered, just as carefully. It seemed the easiest way to put it. No need to mention her bungled role as avenging angel just yet, perhaps not ever. 'So yes, I can safely say I know the guy.'

Katie put her glass down on the table and cleared her throat. 'In that case— Listen, Caro, this isn't going to be easy for me, but—' Her eyes were overbright, her lips shaking, pressed tightly together. 'I made a huge fool of myself,' she muttered. 'I thought I was in love with him at one time. And I really did think he cared for me.'

She was describing circles on the top of the table with the tip of her index finger, her voice so low Caro had to strain to hear her reply when she asked, 'Where did you meet him? You never told me. I wouldn't have thought you moved in the same circles.'

'We don't. Didn't. It was at Gran's birthday party. Her eightieth. You couldn't make it because you came down with flu. Remember? Finn got roped in because he'd come down about Gran's investments and stuff. I got this monumental crush on him and I suspect I made a nuisance of myself. And he was kind, and I mistook it for something else and—'

'He was kind?' Caro interrupted. 'You mean he didn't actually seduce you?'

'No!' Deep colour flooded Katie's face again. 'Did I give you that impression? I must have done. To be truthful, I don't remember him ever touching me.'

Speechless, Caro stared into her sister's pink face. She still looked breathtakingly sweet, young for her years, but the wide, childish innocence of her eyes had been replaced by something more adult, stronger, tougher. She had, Caro suspected, finally grown up.

'The torn blouse,' Caro reminded her. 'Did it tear itself, or did you mistake that for something else?'

She would never have been able to talk to the pre-Dave Katie like that, not if she'd wanted to avoid floods of tears and whole days of hurt silence. It was a measure of her sister's new maturity that she was able, after searching through her memory banks, to offer, 'Grief! You thought he'd torn it off me! I got mugged. Look, I'd better start at the beginning.' She finished the wine in her glass and helped herself to some more. 'Gran's party. All those wrinklies, moaning about their ailments. Nobody talked to me. Mum was helping Mrs F and Polly with the food. I tried to help, for something to do, but I just got in the way. And Finn was there, like I said, trying not to look bored to death. I thought he was the most gorgeous thing I'd ever seen. And he actually spent time with me, talked to me, admired the floral decorations I'd done and said I could, if I wanted, do it professionally. He really made me feel special, as if I had something to offer.'

Caro could understand that. He had the knack of making a girl feel very special indeed. Add to that Katie's desperately low self-esteem—deepened by Gran's continual carping—and the way she'd always seemed to inhabit a dream world of her own making, and everything began to make sense of a kind.

'He said that I had a talent and should use it, and mentioned that there were plenty of hostesses in London and the Home Counties who paid the earth for someone to provide floral decorations for their dinner parties; so, well, I went up to London a time or two and dropped by his offices and asked his advice about setting up in that kind of business on my own—'

'Were you serious about that?'

'Of course not!' Katie raked her fingers through her hair. 'Oh, I dare say I thought I was at the time. But it was just an excuse to be with him, to get his attention. And he was good at that—giving me attention. He'd take me to lunch and give me all sorts of what was probably extremely sound advice—none of which I took.

'I just wanted to talk about it because it gave me the excuse to be near him. Then came the last time we met. I arrived at his office, uninvited, needless to say, and he saw me briefly and told me he'd given me all the advice he could. I was shattered. Oh, he was very nice about it but it didn't make any difference. I was still shattered! Instead of a cosy lunch with the man I loved, with him giving me one hundred per cent of his attention, I was back on the street, on my own, and to cap it all I got mugged!'

Too cross to sit still and listen to any more of this, and frankly appalled, Caro jumped up and tugged the chintzy curtains across the window. It was getting dark outside now and the lights from the big house could be seen glimmering faintly through a belt of trees.

Finn Helliar could very well be behind one of those lit windows. She couldn't bear to be reminded of him—of the things she'd said to him, the dreadful things she'd accused him of. Of the way he'd kissed her and the way she'd responded... Of the way things might have worked out if only...

Oblivious of all that simmering rage, Katie was saying penitently, 'Naturally, I ran straight back to Finn. His secretary got him out of a meeting, and naturally—though I didn't see it that way then—he took me back to his flat and asked his secretary to buy a blouse to replace my ripped one and bring it round.'

She was twisting her hands together in her lap, her eyes embarrassed, avoiding Caro's. 'I honestly thought he'd taken me to his home rather than sort me out back at the office because I was special to him. God, I was too naive to be true! When I think back to it now I loathe myself! I wouldn't let him call the police—my handbag had been stolen but there was nothing much in it, just my fare home and bits and bobs of make-up. And then I got hysterical when he told me he'd phone Mum and get her to drive in and fetch me home.

'I really lost it then. I didn't want to be fetched anywhere—I wanted to stay there with him. And told him so, told him I loved him and hurled myself at him. He was quite probably horrified.'

'I can imagine,' Caro said through her teeth.

She loomed over her sister. She couldn't bring herself to sit down at the table with her right now. 'You didn't try to drown yourself, did you? What you said led me to believe you did and you let me go on thinking it.'

'I'm sorry,' Katie muttered miserably. 'Looking back, it all seems so stupid. That day, the day I got mugged, Finn put me in a cab and sent me home. Mum was out. I got changed and went out, walking aimlessly, and ended up at the lake, of all places. It was evening by then—dusk. Dave came out of the woods, on the track. He was walking his dogs. He called out to me—just "Hi there", you know—but I turned away quickly. I didn't want him to see I'd been crying. I lost my footing and fell in. I felt so stupid. And when you thought I'd done it deliberately, well—' she pulled in a huge, anguished breath '—it seemed more, well, romantic, and—'

'Don't say anything more,' Caro bit out. 'I'm going to bed. I might be able to bring myself to exchange a civil word with you in the morning. There again, I might not.'

The way she was feeling right now, she never wanted to have to speak to her sister again!

CHAPTER TWELVE

'So I'm not at all sure when he'll be back,' Lucy Helliar apologised as she closed the door between the suite and the vestibule, and Caro, trying not to scream with frustration, found a smile and obeyed the invitation to step right along in.

'Some unforeseen legal business cropped up in Paris—involving solicitors and the record company Fleur was with and re-issues and everything getting tied up so that any future income goes to Sophie,' Lucy explained. 'I don't understand the ins and outs of it myself, but it seemed complicated and urgent so he had to drop everything and fly over.'

The compulsion to apologise to Finn had been too strong to deny but it had taken all her courage to bring herself to actually face him. And now Lucy was telling her he was in France, had been for the last eight days.

In the main living room Sophie, with Horn sitting solemnly at her side on the apple-green carpet, was loudly 'reading' a rag book held upside down, but the baby babble turned to a crow of delight as she turned and spied Caro, holding out her arms to be picked up and cuddled.

Caro obliged, annoyed by the lump that jumped into her throat. It was over two weeks since she'd last seen Sophie and she'd missed her more than she would ever have believed possible.

'I guess you'll be relieved to hear everything went smoothly as far as Mytton Wells is concerned. Finn pulled strings and contracts were exchanged the day before he flew to Paris. You should all be comfortably settled in soon. Finn tells me the house is structurally sound as a bell—it just needs re-decorating and the few bits and pieces the previous owners left behind need moving out.'

Lucy bobbed around the room, picking up Sophie's scattered toys, tidying them away. Caro thought she looked relieved to have an adult to talk to after her solitary baby-minding stint.

'I'm not saying that this hotel isn't enormously comfortable, of course. And it's so handy for the park for Sophie's outings, and the staff couldn't be more accommodating, but it's not like a proper home of your own, is it? Now, would you like me to ring for tea, or shall we have it later when Sophie has hers? And tell me how your poor mother is. Are you sure you're happy to leave her? You mustn't feel you have to hurry back on my account.'

Caro declined the offer of tea, began to think seriously about Lucy's final remark, and sat down on one of the sofas with the baby on her knee. She reassured her hostess about her mother's condition.

'Mum's been out of hospital for a few days now and she's feeling much, much better. Her ribs are still strapped and giving her some discomfort but, as she says, that's nothing to what it could have been. And my sister's taken time off work to look after her.'

She and Katie had had several more long talks over the last couple of weeks and Caro had gradually been able to come to terms with what her sister had done, and forgiven her.

And when she'd phoned through to her partner Mary had said, 'Of course you must take time off until poor Emma's home and well on the way to recovery. Do give her my love. Does Finn Helliar want someone to replace you? Should I contact him?'

'If he does, he'll contact you. But don't hold your breath,' Caro had said drily. She would give Mary the news of her ignominious dismissal some other time. 'Why didn't you tell me he was widowed and had travelled back to England with his mother?'

'Didn't I? Goodness. I suppose it must have shot out of my head when you insisted on being interviewed for the position of nanny,' Mary had defended.

So now all that was left was the truly desperate need to put things right with Finn. He wasn't here, of course, and it might be days more before he was back in England, but if she wasn't very much mistaken Lucy was opening a door on a golden opportunity—provided she was brave enough, or devious enough, to take it.

'Well, if you're absolutely sure?'

'About coming back?'

She held her breath and felt her heart thump about in her chest and only expelled a long, slow sigh when Lucy affirmed, 'Yes. Exactly. Of course I was—and still am if it's necessary—perfectly happy to look after little Sophie until Finn can get back from France. But I don't have too much time left in Great Britain and I would like to finish that visit with my friends—but only if you're absolutely sure you are able to leave your mother and pick up your duties here again.'

Her assumptions had been right! Finn hadn't told his mother he'd sacked the nanny. She couldn't imagine why. There was a lot to Finn Helliar she didn't understand. And stuff about herself she was only just beginning to understand, like the depth of devious behaviour she was capable of and the precise extent of her bravery.

It would be easier if Lucy, dear soul that she was, was out of the way visiting her friends when she finally faced Finn with that apology, but when he discovered what she had done he would not be a happy man.

But that didn't stop her. She took a deep breath, painted on a smile, and said, 'Perfectly sure, Mrs Helliar. So why don't you contact your friends and make whatever arrangements you need to make now?'

He would not be pleased to arrive back in London and find her re-installed as Sophie's nanny. Correction, he would spit tacks! But it would give her the perfect opportunity to try to put things right. To apologise profoundly and to take her leave of him carrying second prize with her.

Not first prize, which would be to hear him say he'd been telling the truth about falling in love with her, but the second prize of his forgiveness, which was, after all, probably more than she deserved.

Caro was sure she was going into a decline, or something remarkably like one. Just three days back as Sophie's nanny and all her clothes hung loosely on her and her cheekbones stuck out like doorknobs.

Three days of wondering if she'd done the right thing, of pushing Sophie's buggy for miles and miles round Regent's Park, of long, long evenings broken only by Lucy's friendly phone call when she checked that they were OK, three days of being too hyped up to do more than pick at her food, of wondering when he'd show up and how she'd face him when he did.

'Shall we do something really exciting today?' she asked Sophie on the morning of the fourth day. 'Let's give the park a miss and have a real day out.'

It looked like being a gorgeous day again, this summer seeming set to break all records. The thought of hanging around the hotel suite, with forays into the park to break the monotony, watching the minutes and hours of the day slide away with still no sign of Finn, was something she'd had more than enough of.

She was enjoying looking after his daughter and was, she knew, getting very good at it. The problem was, each day she grew to love the little girl more, and when the time came for that final goodbye she was sure part of her heart would break.

And she wouldn't be at all surprised if Lucy returned from her visit with her friends before her son got back from that Paris business trip. And that would involve her in making a whole extra heap of embarrassing explanations and deprive her of the opportunity of being alone with him.

'A picnic, huh?' She plucked the tiny girl out of her cot and waltzed with her into the bathroom. 'We'll visit the house Daddy's bought for you, and play in the garden. It's a beautiful house, poppet, and you're a very lucky little girl.'

Her own small runabout was now in Finn's underground parking slot here at the hotel. She had come back to town and collected it from outside her apartment block in Highgate as soon as she'd been sure her mother was going to make a full recovery, driving it back to the lodge so that she and Katie didn't have to take David away from his work to do the hospital run. Presumably Finn had left the off-roader in the long-stay airport car park.

So she could ask the kitchens for a picnic hamper and they could be away within the hour, heading for fresh air and silence and a chance for her to renew her acquaintance with the home that was now his, imprint it more deeply on her mind so that she could picture him there in the years to come.

Which was a pretty slushy sort of thought, especially coming from the brain of one of the coolest operators in the nanny-agency business! She was not a sentimental or slushy person.

Or she hadn't been until recently.

Plucking the baby out of the bath, she wrapped the sturdy little body in a huge fluffy towel and squatted back on her heels, her eyes misty, her lower lip caught between her teeth.

She was going to have to pull herself together. OK, so he was the first man who had ever made her feel that there could be something in the business of falling in love and tying your life, your whole future, up with another person, needing and loving someone else until that someone else became your whole existence.

But that didn't mean he would be the last man capable of doing that, did it?

A huge lump constricted her throat. She swallowed it roughly. OK, so who was she fooling? Hell could freeze over before she found another man who affected her the way Finn Helliar did. But that didn't mean he could feel the same way about her, did it?

No, he'd made it abundantly clear he couldn't. First off, the sound of his dead wife's name on her lips had horrified him, made him feel he was making love with something utterly repulsive. He'd certainly acted as if that were the case. And then he'd bawled her out and then he'd sacked her.

Then, just to make sure he couldn't like or respect her in a million years, she'd told him exactly why she'd lied her way into his employ. To get revenge. To pay him back for something he hadn't done.

Of course he'd said that that was something they were going to have to talk about—like when she and Katie could expect to be hauled in front of the courts on a charge of slander. But in the end he hadn't bothered. He probably thought that neither of them was worth the expenditure of time and trouble.

Suddenly, it became imperative that she and Sophie get away from here. It was like being in the dentist's waiting room waiting for her name to be called.

A day in the country would soothe her jangling nerves, give her a breathing space, make her better able to calmly make those overdue apologies when he did turn up, impress him with her sincerity.

She dressed them both in hot-weather casual gear. Ice-blue cotton shorts and a toning T-shirt for Sophie, and a gauzy black cotton skirt and white lawn sleeveless blouse for herself, because they were about the coolest things she had with her.

'Should Mr Helliar return before I do,' she instructed the receptionist when she collected the picnic hamper she'd ordered and the baby seat she'd borrowed, 'please tell him that Nanny Farr has taken the baby to Mytton Wells. We aim to be back well in time for the baby's bedtime.'

A hotel porter was needed to help transport everything to the car. It felt as if they were going on safari, Caro thought wildly, eyeing the borrowed baby seat—essential if Sophie was to be strapped in safely—and the hamper which looked big enough to hold food for five thousand and two bulging bags stuffed with all the bits and pieces Sophie would need during the day, not forgetting Horn.

An hour later, feeling slightly more relaxed, Caro stopped the car under the shade of a group of beech trees at the side of the long drive that wound its endless way up to Mytton Wells.

She had no intention of going on up to the house; it would be locked and empty so there really was no point. But transporting all the paraphernalia, plus Sophie, down to the meadow so that the little girl could run and play in freedom and safety proved more problematical than she'd bargained for.

The time they'd visited before there had been two adults to fetch and carry from the car, two adults to keep an eye on and amuse the lively toddler. She didn't want to think about that day. Thinking about it now made her want to cry.

It had been an almost perfect day, a happy day. Looking back, she now knew she'd been falling in love with him and had already known, deep in the silent places of her heart, that he couldn't be as unprincipled and callous as she'd set out believing him to be.

'Right, Sophie, off we go!' she uttered with a false brightness that was perilously close to tears. Fiercely promising herself she could not get maudlin, she settled the cotton sun-hat more securely on the golden curls. 'You can carry Horn while I push this. OK?'

'This' was a teetering edifice made up of the picnic hamper and the bulging bags of Sophie's necessaries, all balanced precariously on the baby buggy. It took some careful manoeuvring, especially when they'd left the mown expanse of the lower-garden lawns and were negotiating the semi-steep ha-ha that separated meadow and woodland from the more formal areas.

'There! It was worth it, wasn't it, poppet?' Hot and breathless, Caro sank down at last in the long feathery grass which was ornamented with swaying field poppies and ox-eye daisies and rummaged in the picnic basket.

As she'd suspected, the hotel kitchens had packed enough to feed an army. Sophie snacked on fruit and juice and Caro took the top off a plastic container of tiny smoked salmon sandwiches then put it back on again. She wasn't hungry.

So she and Sophie made daisy chains, or rather she did the making while Sophie toddled around pulling up handfuls of flowers until Caro insisted they had enough. She didn't want to denude the meadow of wild flowers entirely!

It was getting hotter, a heavier, more sultry heat, when, an hour or two later, Caro carried the little girl back from their expedition down to the edge of the shallow stream that wound around the bottom of the meadow then disappeared into the wood.

The exercise and fresh air had tired the baby and after giving her another drink of juice Caro settled her and Horn on the cot blanket and the tiny pillow she'd brought along with all the other necessaries. 'Shall we have a story?' She smiled into the already drooping eyes. 'How about Goldilocks? It's your favourite.'

Too late, she was afraid she'd said the wrong thing. Sophie needed to nap and any mention of bears was usually enough to have her racketing around on her hands and knees making her famous growly noises.

But the sudden brightening of those drowsy eyes wasn't the prelude to a game of bears, she realised as the little girl held out her chubby arms and carolled excitedly, 'Daddeeee!'

'How's my sweetie-pie?' Strong, tanned arms scooped the tiny girl up from her nest in the long, soft grasses. His white business-wear shirt had the sleeves rolled up and narrow-fitting dark grey tailored trousers skimmed long, long legs and those lean, mean hips of his.

Caro's fingers dug into the soft, warm grass. She felt dizzy, the sudden shock of seeing him here, where she surely hadn't expected him, blocking the supply of oxygen to her brain.

He joined her, sitting cross-legged on the grass, his baby daughter held firmly between his knees. 'I got your message from Reception.' His deep voice was even, almost without intonation. For some reason his very calmness gave her the shivers and she knew exactly why when he told her, 'I'm not raising the roof, but that doesn't mean I'm not furious with you. I don't want to alarm Sophie by yelling at you—'

Or traumatise her for life by taking you by the throat and shaking, hard, Caro tacked on for him inside her head, and shuddered at the look in his eyes. His voice might be calm but those eyes said it all. Contemptuous dislike didn't come near describing what was staring at her from those glittering silver depths.

'How dare you just walk back, take advantage of my absence, lie to my mother, walk out with my child—?'

'I wouldn't harm her!' she began heatedly, but moderated her tone as his brows drew down in an angry scowl. 'I left a clear message.' One he'd acted on immediately, apparently not even bothering to change out of the suit he'd travelled in. He couldn't really imagine that she was so depraved she'd harm a single hair on his darling daughter's golden head, could he?

'And I didn't lie to your mother. Because you hadn't told her I'd been thrown out, she assumed—'

'Then you lied by omission.' Sweetly said, he might have been talking about the weather, remarking on how wonderful it was. But Caro knew better and so did Sophie, judging by the way she went red in the face and began to bellow.

Finn rose to his feet, rocking his child in his arms, making soothing noises as he tried to pacify the overheated, over-tired infant, but his strong, angular features were stamped with contempt as he instructed, 'Pack everything up ready to put in my car. Sophie and I are leaving.' His eyes were slivers of smouldering silver, glittering at her between thick black lashes. 'You found your way here, you can find your way back.'

CHAPTER THIRTEEN

'WE'LL head straight up towards the house,' Finn directed as Caro balanced the second plastic bag on top of the hamper she'd put in the buggy. 'You can wait on the terrace with Sophie while I bring the car up. I left it directly behind yours on the drive.'

She could imagine him leaping out of the vehicle, striding around until he'd located them, and now he couldn't wait to take his daughter and get away from her!

Heading straight up and across the belt of meadowland towards the paths and lawns of the formal gardens would eventually make for easier going than the route she had taken previously. And waiting outside the house with the baby while he went on his own down the long, long drive to bring his car up made a lot of sense. But it also made her feel small and lost and lonely.

Would he unbend sufficiently to offer her a lift down to where she'd left her car, or would he simply leave her where she was? The mood he appeared to be in, she wouldn't put bets on him doing the former!

Thankfully, Sophie had quietened down, her hot, tear-stained little face turned into her father's shoulder, the occasional hiccup and sniffle the only remnants of her earlier bawling session.

Finn probably had the gall to blame her for the noisy outburst, Caro grouched to herself as she dragged the laden buggy over the meadow, when in reality it was all down to him, for popping up out of the blue and making the little girl over-excited when she, Caro, had got her nicely ready to nap. She really hated to think that the child had been in any way affected by the veiled antagonism between her father and her nanny.

Staring at his impressively broad, retreating back, enraged by his high-handed attitude, she rubbed the back of her hand over her perspiring forehead and both the bags fell off the buggy, leaking towels and baby cream, disposable nappies, changes of clothing and baby wipes in every direction.

Her howl of frustration brought him striding straight back to her and if she hadn't been feeling so hot and bothered she knew the ice of his eyes would have given her frostbite.

'Give that lot to me.' He held out a commanding hand, his brows knitting with dark impatience. 'There's a storm about to break, or hadn't you noticed?'

Never mind the ominously darkening sky, the thick, still stickiness of the air—the real storm was happening right inside her.

She tossed him a glowering look of sheer resentment and he said brusquely, 'Take Sophie. Head up for the house.' And he carefully placed the now sleeping child in her arms and bent to retrieve all the scattered bits and pieces.

The first drops of rain hit as she hurried along the path between the double herbaceous borders. Huge drops, falling slowly at first and then fast and furiously so that she was forced to bend almost double to prevent Sophie from getting soaked as well.

Thunder was growling and prowling around the heavy skies and Finn brushed past her, seemingly having abandoned the burdened baby buggy, took her by the waist and hustled her up the steps to the terrace, pushing her and the baby beneath the slight shelter of the eaves while he fished a keyring from his trouser pocket and opened the tall French windows.

'Get inside,' he instructed tersely. 'We'll wait the storm out here.' He disappeared back into the deluge and Caro stepped through the glass doors and into the dim and empty room.

Not quite empty, though. A battered three-piece suite, a couple of mismatched bookcases—homemade, by the amateurish look of them, out of flimsy wood—and several cardboard boxes full of things wrapped in newspaper were piled up against one wall of the high-ceilinged, elegantly proportioned room.

When they'd viewed the property for the first time Finn had looked at the unwanted remnants of someone else's life and said wryly, 'It's amazing what people will hoard, isn't it? According to the estate agent these are the things the house-clearance people wouldn't look at when the owner sold up before moving to a retirement home.'

What a long time ago that seemed. A different life. Yet it wasn't. They were different people. That was what had changed—the people they were and the way they viewed each other.

Caro shivered, her wet clothes sticking to her body, and Finn walked back through the French windows, wetter by far, soaked to the skin. He dumped the picnic hamper and the two plastic bags on the floor. 'Is there anything amongst that lot we could wrap her in?'

'A woolly blanket.' Her mouth was so dry she could barely speak. He was making her nervous. He didn't look as if he'd listen to an apology coming from her, let alone accept it. And she had the uneasy suspicion that if he hadn't needed her to hold his sleeping daughter while he rummaged in the bags for that blanket she would have been out of his house, deluge or no deluge, and splashing down the drive to her car.

Finn located the blanket and strode over to the pile of unwanted furniture, swinging one easy chair around to face the other, pushing them together to create a makeshift bed, then jerked his head in Caro's direction, not speaking to her because he couldn't—not, he feared, without snarling. And not looking at her either because he couldn't—not without wanting her.

Fortunately, there was no need to issue instructions. She joined him and gently placed Sophie on her back in the confined chair space. This close, he could smell the elusive perfume that he remembered as being the seductive essence of her, could hear the whisper of her shallow breathing.

He covered his daughter with the blanket then felt every bone in his body lock with tension when the minx at his side reached out a hand and touched his arm.

'Don't you want to know why I hung around, waiting until you came back from France?'

'Not particularly.' He stepped away and watched

her hand fall back to her side. Perversely, his skin burned where her cool fingers had touched him. 'It would probably give me nightmares.'

The rain had plastered her hair to her beautifully shaped head, moulded the fine cotton of her clothes to that exquisite, graceful body. Finn gritted his teeth. This close, this woman was in danger of sending him out of his mind.

This woman had blamed him for something he hadn't done, and lied and schemed to get close to him, using sweet, innocent little Sophie, and this same woman had brought him to the point of believing himself in love with her!

How could his character judgement be so out of kilter? How could he have wanted to spend the rest of his life with someone so irrational, so blinkered?

And, worse yet, there was the sheer absurdity of believing himself in love—and for the first time in his entire adult life—with a woman who had used her sex as a weapon, allowed herself to share sexual intimacies with a man she had believed to be married in order to punish him for something he hadn't done!

This was a woman to be avoided at all costs!

'I needed to apologise to you—'

'You did? Now, I wonder why? Because you are devious, because you were hell-bent on revenge—a despicable thing, revenge, or don't you think so? Or because you don't bother to ask questions, just appoint yourself judge, jury and executioner—?'

'Don't!' Her voice was thick with misery, her golden eyes sparkling with sudden, unshed tears. Her obvious distress unsettled him.

He moved away from the soundly sleeping baby,

gravitated to the French windows and stared out at the drenching rain, at the distant flashes and flickers of lightning.

'I want to say I'm sorry—desperately sorry—for believing the things Katie said about you.'

Her smooth brow furrowed. It was difficult to apologise to someone who couldn't be bothered to listen. His back was turned to her, the rain-sodden fabric of his shirt clinging to those wide, rangy shoulders. She felt excluded, a pariah, and probably justifiably, she concluded mournfully.

'But I've got to admit I did believe them—to begin with, that is,' she tried again. 'Then, when I got to know you better, and I…' She couldn't possibly confess her true feelings for him; she wasn't that courageous. 'And like you, I really doubted you could have done what she'd accused you of.'

'Seduced a child. What was she at the time? Seventeen? With a mental and emotional capacity of a ten-year-old,' he said flatly. 'You shared mine and Sophie's lives, believing I was that type of bastard.' That hurt.

'Not for long.' Her voice shook. 'I believed it before I met you because Katie had told me it was so. Though, to be absolutely fair, she never once said that you took her to bed, or that she attempted to drown herself after she learned you'd married Fleur Ferrand who was then carrying your child: Sophie.

'She didn't exactly say those things, not in so many words, but they were implied and for some reason best known to herself—maybe because it made her feel she was the centre of attention—she allowed me to go on believing the lies.'

He turned, his eyes bleak, and she said thinly, 'That makes Katie sound dreadful. And it's not as simple as that. Very few things in life are really simple—you don't need me to tell you that. But I do know that Katie truly did believe she was in love with you, and because you had shown an interest in her, made time for her, taken her to lunch—certainly at that time the only man who ever had—she talked herself into believing her own fantasies.

'And I've always looked after her, stuck up for her against Gran—who can be terrifying—because she's never been able to stick up for herself; she's too timid. She's always been lonely, too shy to make friends. So I've always protected her because there was no one else to do it. Mum's too fond of a quiet life to want to make waves. And by taking the job of Sophie's nanny I thought I would have the time to find a way to pay you back. For that I am truly, deeply sorry.'

He looked at her with desolate eyes. He walked back into the body of the room, putting distance between them. She sounded sincere but how could he trust her? Why should he even want to? And she was shivering. From being chilled, or from nervous tension? Did he even care?

Schooling all expression from his features, all emotion from his voice, he said, 'Apology noted and accepted. Now may we forget it? The subject's distasteful. I take it there's food in that hamper? Could you investigate while I look for something to burn in the hearth to help us get dry?'

Thunder cracked, closer now, and the rain poured relentlessly down the window-panes. They could be sheltering here for quite some time, he thought grimly, and strode out of the room, going in search of the dusty-looking matchbox that he vaguely remembered seeing lying on the floor of one of the box rooms when they'd viewed the property for the first time.

He would never forget that day. Something warm and sweet had tugged at his heart, something that had said they were a family. It had certainly felt that way, as if they belonged together.

It had been a day of bitter disillusionment, too. He would never forget that, either.

The matchbox was probably empty, just another piece of debris the house-clearance people had neglected to remove, but it gave him the excuse to get out of that room, away from her, away from the stupid, self-destructive yearning to take her in his arms and make love to her until they were both too exhausted to move, let alone think.

He took the stairs two at a time, the release of energy not doing as much as it should to restore his mind to a more peaceful state. For the first time ever he could well imagine what it would feel like to have an addictive personality, to crave something you knew darn well was bad for you!

The box held two matches, one spent, the other live. Finn almost felt like smiling. Trying to make a fire would give him something to do. It could be as much as an hour before Sophie woke and helped to defuse the tension just by being her cute and demanding small self.

He collected the ramshackle bookcases and carried them through to the back where the noise of their breaking wouldn't disturb Sophie. They broke into pieces like the painted orange boxes they had obviously been made from and with the help of some rumpled sheets of newspaper, taken from the packing cases, and the single match, he was able to sit back on his heels and spend a satisfying few moments watching the flames leap up his own chimney.

'Couldn't you get clapped in irons for burning someone else's property?'

'They can always try suing!' He had heard the note of humour in her voice—albeit a slightly wistful one—and responded in kind. 'Though I guess the burning of antique orange boxes, covered in old brown paint, could be headline material. Come closer.' He stood up, moving so that the warmth from the flames could reach her. But she just stood where she was, her face a pale blur in the dim, rainy light. She was still shivering.

Half impatiently, he reached out and circled her wrist with his thumb and forefinger. 'Come. Closer to the fire.' Her skin was so cool, her bones so fragile. The combination made his heart lurch with unexpected tenderness. Women were popularly supposed to be the nurturing sex but right now all he wanted to do was keep her safe and warm, provide comfort and ease.

He tugged her into the circle of the firelight, an exploratory hand sliding over her back. As he had thought, the sleeveless cotton top was still soaking wet; he had seen the way she'd curved her body protectively around Sophie as she'd run through the downpour.

Huge golden eyes were fixed unwaveringly on his

face as he touched her and she was still shaking, inner tension intensifying the tremors, affecting him too, making his fingers shake as he slowly began to undo the row of tiny fabric-covered buttons that marched down the front of her top.

Affected his voice, too, making it emerge thickly, as if he hadn't used it in a long, long while, when he explained, 'You'll catch a chill if you stay in these wet things any longer.'

The back of his hand brushed the taut swell of one breast, daintily covered—or nearly so—in the finest of laces and silks. He heard the inward tug of her breath, felt the smooth heat of her skin and felt his legs go weak, his stomach muscles clench with a fire that spread in a wild explosion of need, engulfing his loins, every last part of his body.

Now all he wanted to do was stroke her, pleasure her, possess her.

And she, the witch, knew that, and began to draw on the magic she possessed to make it so, soft dark lashes fluttering against her ivory cheeks as she bent her head to watch her fingers tug his shirt from the waistband of his trousers then move to the buttons, her breath coming in quick, shallow beats, her breasts taut, swollen, rosy in the fireglow.

His hands moved to her shoulders, whether to hold her away or to keep her close he couldn't be sure. His head was reeling, his mind a blank. He wasn't sure of anything until her small hands parted the sodden fabric of his shirt and her soft palms rested against his ribs. And then there was no doubt. None at all.

He needed this woman with an intensity that overwhelmed him, with a hedonistic abandonment that testified to the power of her sorcery, and the blood roared through his veins, the drum-beat deafening him as her hands slid smoothly up to his shoulders, easing the wet fabric away from his body.

Caro drew in a jagged breath, holding it, hardly daring to exhale as tiny tremors of exquisite sensation trickled through her when her fingers stroked the warm, oiled satin of his skin.

His acceptance of her apology had been curt and cold to the point of total indifference, and he'd left the room as if he couldn't bear to be anywhere near her.

But now—now that he'd touched her, looked at her with naked desire in those sexy silver eyes—now maybe everything would be all right. She moved closer, sliding her body against his, wound her slender arms around his neck and lifted her face to his.

His warm lips lightly covered hers, tasting her, the tip of his tongue outlining the shape of her mouth, dipping inside until she opened to him, moaning her need to accept him utterly.

And when the kiss deepened to a passionate intensity that left her reeling, clinging to him, she responded with a hunger that matched his own. She loved him, was in love with him, and even if things didn't work out she would have this.

This…and more… Sensations bombarded her, leaving her weak and giddy, breathless and clinging as his hands fastened on her hips, pulling her against his body, leaving her in no doubt at all about the extent of his arousal, one of his thighs nudging hers apart, making her shock all the greater when he suddenly stepped back, his chest heaving as if each breath was torture.

'God help me—but you send me insane!'

'Finn!' Caro gasped his name. She felt as if she'd been pushed out in the cold, away from light and love and hope, the fallen angel banished from heaven. Her breath bunched in her lungs, hurting, her eyes filled with tears, stinging.

His voice was low, raw. 'Sophie could wake at any moment. I should congratulate you. No other woman has ever come near making me forget my child!'

He turned abruptly, dragging the old sofa closer to the fire, draping her top and his shirt over the end to dry.

Caro put her hands up to her burning cheeks. Sophie. Of course. The tiny girl napped for an hour every afternoon. Rarely any longer than that. Which meant she'd soon be waking, needing her nappy changing, wanting a drink and maybe one of the sand-wiches.

That both she and Finn had overlooked the pos-sibility of her waking at any moment just went to show how far they'd been carried away, absorbed in each other. She took her top and held it closer to the leaping flames, watching the steam rise gently from her skirt. She felt absurdly shy, although her bra was perfectly respectable. It was because there was still an edginess between them.

'Finn?'

He had gone to stand at the windows, watching the weather. The storm was passing, the sky lighter, the rain less heavy.

'Well?'

The touch of impatience in his voice made her suck her lower lip between her teeth. Somehow they had to get things straightened out. She had to know if there was any chance at all of things working out between them. She wouldn't weep and wail if he told her there wasn't. She would accept it, with dignity, and cut her losses. Or try to.

She cleared her throat. 'When we were here before...' They had become absorbed in each other that time, too. Lost to everything but the way they could make each other feel. 'You said...' God, but this was difficult. And he wasn't making it easier, the rigid line of his back, the way it was turned on her hurtfully dismissive. 'You said you thought you were falling in love with me,' she pushed out bravely. 'Did you mean it? It wasn't just a line you use to get a woman into your bed?'

Sweat broke out on her short upper lip at his dry riposte. 'I don't normally have to go quite that far.'

'I can believe it.' Was that her voice, so thick and heavy? She wished he would turn and look at her when he spoke; she wished he'd smile, reassure her, let her feel she wasn't about to make a monumental fool of herself.

'I want you to have meant it...I... You see, I was falling in love with you, too.' She held her breath, hardly daring to breathe or to hope, and he did turn then, but slowly, swinging round on the balls of his feet, his austere features unreadable.

'Oh, yes? Make a habit of it, do you? Falling in love with married men—making love with married men?'

His scorn flayed her. She moistened her dry lips

with the tip of her tongue and held her crumpled cotton top in front of her. 'You're not a married man,' she croaked miserably.

'You thought I was. At the time. Which comes to the same thing, at least from the point of view of where you stood a couple of weeks ago.'

'I wouldn't have let things go any further.' Caro pulled on the nearly dry cotton top, fastening the buttons with fingers that felt like a row of swollen thumbs. Whatever she said she was digging a pit to bury herself in. 'It had been my idea of a fitting revenge but—'

'Cruel as well as devious!' he taunted, then snagged his hand through his rapidly drying hair, making it stick up in endearing tufts. He walked across the room to check on Sophie. The baby was beginning to stir, kicking her legs under the blanket. 'I think you should go,' Finn said. 'The storm's passed over; it's barely raining at all. I was told you'd borrowed a baby seat from the hotel. I'll make sure it's returned—put it in the Range Rover, would you? It is unlocked.'

He bent and plucked his now gurgling baby daughter out of her makeshift cot and held her against his broad, naked chest.

And Caroline Farr walked out into the soft summer rain and let the tears she'd vowed she wouldn't shed pour down her face.

CHAPTER FOURTEEN

CARO checked the dashboard clock again. She was going to be late.

A family dinner at eight at the big house, during which, apparently, Gran would break some important news, followed by a sedate drinks and nibbles party for family and friends to celebrate Katie and David's engagement.

Caro didn't really want to be in on either event. It was three weeks since Finn had pushed her out of his life and she was still feeling wounded and raw, in no mood for parties or one of Gran's interminable dinners. But she hadn't been able to make up an excuse when her mum had phoned the invitation through.

'They delayed the engagement party until I was back on my feet again—wasn't that sweet of them? And Gran's surprise is a biggy, I can promise you that. But my lips are sealed. I promised. But you know, she's changed. She's much softer lately. I never thought I'd see the day when I forgot to be frightened of my mother-in-law!'

At least that was something positive, Caro thought as she drove past the lodge on the way up to the big house. And there it was, a huge Gothic pile drowsing in the early evening sun.

She left her car alongside David's and sent up a brief prayer of thankfulness because her sister had found someone who would keep her feet firmly on the ground and her head out of the clouds.

The main door at the head of the wide flight of stone steps was open, the vast hall empty, dim and echoing. She heaved a sigh. Dinner at eight. It was already twenty past. Time and Gran waited for no one, she misquoted in her head, and went through to the great polish-smelling, mahogany-dark dining room.

Her grandmother said, 'You are exactly twenty minutes and thirty seconds late. What kept you?'

'The traffic, Gran.' And the manifestly dreary inability to rouse herself to do anything more than plod through each interminable day and endless night. 'Sorry, everyone.'

Her mother and Katie were looking party-pretty and Gran, as usual, dominated the gathering both with the strength of her personality and her patrician looks. Yet David, spruced up, his hair neat, his wide shoulders covered by a commendably fine lightweight jacket, looked as if he could hold his own with the old lady, no trouble at all.

'We forgive you,' the matriarch granted before ruining the gracious tone entirely. 'Everything's cold. So help yourself from the sideboard and make sure you have enough. You've lost weight and look dreadful. Your clothes are hanging off you. Most unbecoming. Are you ill? Or is the baggy look the latest fashion?'

Caro shrugged. OK, so she had got to be a bag of bones in hardly any time at all and nothing fitted, least of all the ivory silk shirtwaister she'd uninterestedly buttoned herself into this evening. And she knew Gran used rudeness to mask the way she cared but no way was she about to break down in tears and confess that she was pining away for the only man in the world she could ever love.

'I don't think so. But I knew Mum and Katie would be looking like princesses and I didn't want to out-shine you as well!' She grinned at her grandmother and saw her eyes twinkle in response.

'*Touché*, young lady! Now, fill your plate. The sooner we've all finished eating, the sooner you will hear my news. And you are all going to like what you hear. Isn't that so, Emma?'

As Caro helped herself sparingly from the selection of cold meats and salads she marvelled at how perky her mother sounded. She was chattering about the coming party, who had been invited, what they would be given to eat, and how she and Katie had spent all day helping Mrs Fairchild prepare the food.

In the past Elinor Farr had had nothing but scorn for her 'wishy-washy' daughter-in-law and the more scorned Emma had been, the more wishy-washy she had become, hardly daring to open her mouth in her formidable mother-in-law's presence.

It had been a vicious circle. But, fingers crossed, Caro thought, smiling across the table at David as he poured wine for her, the circle was broken.

'The party guests will start arriving in half an hour so we'll have coffee in the small drawing room,' Elinor said after the summer pudding had been re-duced to crumbs. 'The Fairchilds and Polly will be joining us—what I have to say affects them, too. And Finn Helliar should be already waiting, I think. I in-vited him to have dinner with us, but he made some excuse and declined.'

There was general movement as everyone got to their feet. Apart from Caro who was solidly glued to her chair. There was a roaring sound in her ears and she wondered hazily if she was about to faint for the first time in her life and whether everyone would come rushing back and make her put her head between her knees.

'I'll see if Mrs Fairchild has brought the coffee through,' Emma said, obviously unaware that her elder daughter was in shock. 'If not, I'll give her a hand. We don't have a lot of time.' And she followed Katie and her brand-new fiancé out of the door.

'Close your mouth, Caroline. Drink the rest of your wine if you're in need of Dutch courage,' Elinor said into the very heavy silence. 'Then you may escort me to the drawing room.'

Caro swallowed raggedly. 'What is Finn Helliar doing here?' Besides haunting her, reminding her of what she wanted and couldn't have.

'Apart from doing all the donkey-work—and here I'm talking about the news I'm about to give you all—he asked if he might come. He needs to talk to you.' Her eyes glittered with mischief. 'About a nanny for that little daughter of his, perhaps? Ah.' She leaned more heavily on her stick and poked her face closer to Caro's. 'I know all about that little escapade. Or as much as Finn Helliar thought fit to tell me. I suspect he left the more outrageous bits out of his narrative, not realising that I'm completely unshockable. Well, are you coming? Or have you turned into a coward since I saw you last?'

That did it. Caro swallowed the wine in her glass,

shot to her feet and offered her arm to her grandmother.

She would face Finn Helliar, hear what he had to
say—which, she had no doubt at all, would be something about her devious nature, her incompetence, and
quite possibly about his intention to sue Grandes
Familles for misrepresentation or whatever, and
would make quite unpleasant hearing. But she would
do it. No one would ever have cause to call her a
coward!

And then she would slip away from the party and
go home and restart the process of putting him right
out of her heart and mind and hope she found it easier
second time around.

She was aware that she and her grandmother made
quite an entrance, that the family and the indoor
staff—the Fairchilds and Pol—were seated and wearing their most expectant faces, and that Finn stood
over by the windows, his back to what was left of the
evening light so that she couldn't have seen his face
properly even if she'd wanted to, which she didn't.

While Elinor seated herself in an elaborately
carved, high-backed chair that was suspiciously remi-
niscent of a throne and regally waved aside Pol's offer
of coffee, Caro stood by the door, ready to make a
rapid departure as soon as she possibly could, conscious, horribly, of Finn's eyes on her but steadfastly
refusing to look his way.

If he wanted to talk to her then he would have to
approach her, not the other way around. She wasn't
in the habit of going out of her way to look for heartache—and in this case it would be more heartache
than she could handle.

Her grandmother was talking but Caro couldn't hear what she was saying; her heart was beating such a loud, heavy tattoo, it drowned out everything else.

Until the sound of Finn's name sliced through the thunderous racket. 'Finn Helliar's father helped my husband set up all these trusts many years ago and Finn himself was kind enough to agree to set about the arduous task of unravelling them.

'Two events were instrumental in my decision. Katie almost drowned, and would have done had my future grandson-in-law not jumped in and pulled her out of the lake, and Emma could so easily have been killed or maimed for life in a road traffic accident. I realised then how much these two people really mean to me. Playing the matriarch and watching people jump when I pulled their strings became totally unimportant for the first time in my very long life.'

Elinor Farr fell silent. No one spoke. Caro was aware of Finn watching her from across the room. The intentness, the steadiness of his scrutiny made the air fizz. She wanted out, but couldn't move. She would just have to endure and wait until he decided to come out with whatever it was he felt he had to say to her.

'So...' Elinor looked into each face in turn. 'This house, this estate, is to be sold. All the family assets are to be liquidised. Dora and Bert—' she smiled at the Fairchilds '—and you too, dear Polly, will have what is due to you to enjoy without the tedium of waiting for it to appear in my will. The rest will be divided into four equal parts.'

Murmurs of barely suppressed excitement issued from the indoor staff. They were all elderly, had served Gran well, and had earned a peaceful retirement. And Caro could hardly believe that her grandmother was letting so much power slip through her fingers. She had held the reins so long, so tightly...

She must have had all this in mind that day when she'd phoned with the news of Mum's accident. She'd insisted on speaking to Finn, on seeing him...

'Emma and I have decided to travel,' Elinor said, to Caro's total amazement. 'When we find somewhere we really like we'll settle.' And to Katie, who was still looking shell-shocked, she added, 'You and David must do as you see fit with your share, dear. But I have it on good authority that the old Travers' place—the market garden—will shortly be going to auction...'

Caro slipped out of the room. In the excitement, the rapid-fire discussions that were now going on, she wouldn't be missed. She really and truly had meant to stay and hear whatever it was that Finn wanted to say to her but now knew she simply couldn't face it.

So she was a coward after all, but there was precious little she could do about it. It was much too soon after she'd confessed her feelings for him, told him she loved him, then suffered the hurt and humiliation of having him throw her out.

Tears flooded her eyes and thickened her throat as she stumbled blindly across the hall. Call her a coward, but she'd have to be a darn sight stronger emotionally than she was at the moment before she could do as much as stay in the same room with him, never mind hold a one-to-one conversation with him and emerge from the probably acrimonious encounter with any dignity left at all.

'Caro—stop.' The manacle of his hand trapped her

arm. She looked around her wildly. Everywhere was
still and silent, apart from the ragged sound of her
breathing, the manic thumping of her heart. But very
soon now the party guests would begin to arrive and
her immediate escape route would be blocked.

She tried to tug her arm away. 'Please let me go.
I'm leaving. We can talk some other time. Or,' she
tacked on bitterly, 'write me a letter.'

'We talk now.' He was wearing a lightweight pale
grey tailored jacket over a black silk polo shirt. He
looked powerful and menacing and her poor heart
shook. 'But not here.' He strode towards the open
front door and Caro, still manacled, tottered behind
him. 'We're leaving. And before you get any ideas
you're leaving with me, not running away from me.'

His eyes were hooded, hiding his expression as they
fastened on her mouth. His mouth was curved in that
lazy, effortlessly sensual smile that made her feel as
if she was being very thoroughly ravished.

She turned her head swiftly, before he could recog-
nise the yearning in her eyes for what it was. A yearning to be kissed. And the abrupt movement made the
tears that had been giving her eyes a glittering sheen
trickle down her face, and he muttered gruffly,
'Caro—don't!' and swung her up into his arms and
carried her out, popping her in the passenger seat of
the off-roader, which was neatly parked behind her
car, hemming her in so that she couldn't have escaped, not without his say-so.

He was beside her, in the driver's seat, before she
could gather her wits, or the will, to jump straight
back out.

He turned to her, rubbing the traces of moisture

from her cheeks with the ball of his thumb. His touch transfixed her; she could have stayed where she was for ever, letting him touch her. It was as if he had cast a spell over her, robbed her of her will, the power to think for herself. He could turn her into his sex slave—no trouble at all!

Self-destructive madness!

She would have twisted her head away but he moved before she was able to shake herself out of the trance, fastening his seat belt and starting the engine.

'What are you doing?' Was that her voice, that feeble wail?

'Taking you to where we can have some privacy. Fasten your seat belt.'

She did, but only to stop him doing it for her. The lodge came in sight around the bend and she gabbled, 'Stop here. All the privacy you need—they won't be home before midnight!'

He drove on as if she hadn't spoken and she gathered up what was left of her pride and the bits of her spirit that hadn't been crushed and said crossly, 'Look, I know you've got every reason to be annoyed with me, but isn't this taking things a tad too far?'

Being cooped up with him in a moving vehicle was having a disastrous effect on her hormones. Much more of this close proximity and she'd start acting like a fool. Again. She'd done quite enough of that when she'd crawled all over him and told him she loved him! 'Why don't you pull over, say what's bothering you, and be on your way?'

'I am on my way, sweetheart. And you're coming with me. We've got a lot to talk about, and Ma's looking after Sophie in London, and the decorators have moved out of Mytton Wells. There's not much there in the way of home comforts as yet. A bed, a couple of chairs—'

'If you're suggesting what I think you're suggesting—'

'That we spend the night at Mytton getting straightened out. That's about the size of it, yes.' He turned his head, his silver eyes laughing at her. 'And before you start getting righteously indignant, or coming up with a thousand and one reasons for not spending the night with me, just think on.'

The very idea of them spending the night together made her feel like a gutted rag doll. She couldn't think why he'd want to, why he'd go to the trouble of virtually kidnapping her. Unless, of course, he was bored.

He'd had business with her grandmother and had in any case intended to go cross country to his new home, perhaps to check on the decorators' work. So why not take her with him? She'd made it perfectly plain on the afternoon of the thunderstorm that she was very ready and rather more than willing!

So she'd do. Provided, of course, she kept her mouth shut and didn't mention his former wife, because that, as if she didn't know it, was a sackable offence!

The idea of it kept her speechless. Speechless with trying to ignore the lure of the forbidden, the out-of-the-question, the ultimate in temptation—

'When I followed you out of the room back there I had a quick word with your grandmother. I said I was taking you to Mytton, to expect you back when she saw you, and not to worry. You don't have to be in work tomorrow. It's Sunday. So that's sorted. Which leaves us free to sort out what we feel about each other.'

And just how would they do that? In that bed he'd mentioned? She didn't need to be over-endowed in the imagination department to picture it.

What with loving him so madly, her total lack of will-power when he was around with that sexy, sinful smile, those wicked, glinting eyes, she knew exactly what would happen. Knew she'd rapturously consummate her love for him, give him all her loving and then some, and then get thrown off his property if she so much as opened her mouth and said something she shouldn't.

Thanks, but no, thanks.

'We've a way to go,' he said, and whether he meant it in cross-country miles or in reaching some kind of mutual understanding Caro didn't know, and gave up wondering as he told her, 'Ma's happy to look after Sophie in London while I arrange furnishing and part-time staff for Mytton Wells. She'll be in England until the autumn, which is when I'd planned to take up the reins at the bank again, so that gives me time to organise everything this end. I'll work mainly from home, I've decided, so that I can spend as much time as possible around Sophie and whoever's being surrogate mum.'

He meant Sophie's future nanny, of course. It certainly would not be her. That dratted lump clogged up her throat again and she said hoarsely, 'It all sounds quite perfect. But I'm sure you didn't kidnap me to talk about your domestic arrangements.'

'Too right I didn't. And be honest—I didn't kidnap

you, Caro. Instinct tells me you want to be with me; all you needed was a little persuading.'

His instinct was right on the mark, she decided glumly, knotting her fingers together in her lap and wishing he didn't have the ability to look deep into the secrets of her heart.

Of course she could have resisted, told him she refused to go anywhere with him, much less spend the night with him at Mytton. If she'd said it loudly enough, firmly enough, he would have listened. He wasn't a criminal and he wasn't a brute.

He would be remembering her confession of love. She wondered miserably how much mileage he intended to make out of that!

They'd left the motorway and the major roads were behind them and the sturdy vehicle had slowed down in the narrow tangle of lanes. It wouldn't be long before they reached his new home and that would test her emotional strength to the very limit.

Mytton Wells. Twice the scene of her humiliation and pain. Yet it was where she most longed to be. With him. With Sophie. For always.

'I've got a shrewd idea what this is all about. Punishment,' she said gruffly. 'So bawl me out as much as you like—for the stunt I pulled, I fully deserve it. I'd prefer it if you didn't publicly humiliate the agency, but I'll understand if you feel you must. Passing myself off as a competent, trained nanny was unforgivable, unprofessional and immature. I apologise unreservedly.'

It was the nearest she could get to grovelling and did not merit his roar of laughter. 'You find me amusing?' she said frigidly.

He took his eyes off the road for a second and flicked her a wicked glance. 'Amusing, exasperating, sexy, appealing, adorable. And I've no intention of bawling you out, as you put it. And the only damage I'm likely to do to your precious agency is to deprive them of your presence. If I can do the lion's share of my work from an office at home, then so can you.'

Caro stared at his profile. He looked normal. He didn't look like someone who'd suddenly lost it, gone off his trolley.

So it must be her. She must be so emotionally mangled that she was dreaming up impossible scenarios, putting imaginary words into his mouth.

There was only one explanation and that was totally unlikely, and completely out of the question, but she voiced it, just in case. 'Am I to take it that you would like me to continue as Sophie's nanny?'

'Certainly not. I couldn't stand the strain! You said earlier that you thought the set-up at Mytton sounded perfect. You were wrong. But you could make it perfect. Share it with us. Be there with us, as Sophie's mum, as my wife, as mother of my children—if you want them.'

Caro swallowed. Hard. She was dreaming. She had to be. Dusk had deepened into darkness. The headlights carved a tunnel between the high hedgerows. Dreaming, or died and gone to heaven!

'Caro! Say something!' His voice was raw round the edges. 'Dammit, woman! This is impossible!' Frustration growled in his tone. 'I didn't intend proposing at a time when I have to keep both eyes on the road and both hands on the wheel! You dragged it out of me! There's champagne in the fridge at Mytton, and a bed, and—'

'Are you proposing marriage, Finn?' That proved it. She *was* dreaming. She put out a tentative, exploratory hand and rested it on his thigh. The heat of his flesh burned her through the soft, lightweight fabric and felt solidly, sexily real.

'Don't do that!' he muttered hoarsely, and knocked her hand away.

'Do what?' She put her hand on his knee. That, too, felt reassuringly real.

'Touch me,' he growled through his teeth. 'We are a good ten minutes away from Mytton and there are no lay-bys along this lane. And even if there were I do not want to make love with you on a car seat in a lay-by. But if you keep touching me I will not be held responsible.'

How could she believe him?

How could she not believe him and deny herself a taste of heaven? Could hearts break in dreams as well as in reality?

She folded her hands primly in her lap. He had made it sound as if something cataclysmic would happen if she touched him one more time. And he was right. Heat of the wicked, wanton kind was building up right inside her, coiling sweetly, hotly through her, making her ache with longing.

'But you don't like me.' She sounded as puzzled as she was. 'You threw me out.'

'So?' He sounded as if he hurled half-clothed females off his property every day of his life. 'You made me angry. You'd hurt me. I couldn't resist you, and I didn't want to entrust my happiness to the type of woman who would make love with a man she believed to be married, to get revenge for something he hadn't done.'

'I did try to explain about all that, and I have apologised. And before we went to Mytton that first time I'd decided I wouldn't go through with the revenge thing. I was just going to tell you what I thought of what I then believed you'd done to Katie...'

She pushed her hands shakily through her hair. All this was getting weirder by the second. Why would he propose marriage to a woman he didn't like? 'But you touched me, kissed me, and things just got out of hand, and I wasn't thinking about anything but the way it felt to be in your arms and—'

'Don't I know it!' Briefly, emotionally, his hand covered hers in her lap. 'After you'd gone I spent days thinking about it. About us.' He transferred his hand back to the steering wheel. 'I ended up despising myself. I'd blamed you for believing the worst of me without hearing my side of things or going to the trouble to get at the truth.

'Yet there I was doing the same to you, and I had heard your side of the story. Of course you wanted to pay me back for hurting your sister. Of course you believed her story. Why wouldn't you? You'd been standing up for her for most of your life, you loved her, you didn't know me from Adam. So naturally you took up the cudgels on her behalf.

'And once I'd seen that particular light, and come to terms with the way you'd said you'd intended to get revenge, I knew that you weren't the sort of woman to make love with a married man. You stopped me well before we got to the point of no return.'

'I don't know that I understand you.' Her mouth was dry; she could hardly get the words out. 'You fired me—'

'I fired you because I'd been hurt. I'd fallen in love with you and had got to the point of telling you so, and you shattered me completely. You let me know you believed I was married.'

She closed her eyes, pulling oxygen deep into her lungs because she was light-headed. 'You went cold on me, told me your wife was dead. Then sacked me. I thought it was because you still mourned her so much, had loved her so much, you thought hearing her name on my lips was sullying her memory. But it wasn't that? Please say it wasn't. I love you, Finn; I want to be your wife. But I wouldn't want to feel I was a second-rate substitute, not daring to mention her name, seeing a silver-framed photograph of her in every room I went into.'

They were on the Mytton Wells driveway now and the headlights illuminated the façade of the lovely old house. Finn switched off the lights, cut the engine, turned to her and tenderly took her face between his hands.

'I love you, Caroline Farr. More than I've ever loved anyone or anything. I keep Fleur's photographs around so that Sophie will grow up knowing what her mother looked like and will be able to identify with her.' The balls of his thumbs stroked the smooth hollows beneath her cheekbones, then slid slowly down to rest at the corners of her mouth.

'I married Fleur because she was in deep, deep

trouble. It's a long story, sweetheart, and I'll try to keep it brief because sitting here, talking about my first wife, is not something that's top of my wants list right at the moment.

'After my father retired, he and Ma lived in the south of France. Fleur's adoptive mother came in on a daily basis to cook and clean. I was twenty-four to Fleur's fourteen when I met her for the first time. I used to go out there several times a year and got to know Fleur well. She was a determined young lady. She was going to make something of her life; she wasn't going to scratch a living as her parents did. I admired her spirit. She would have been sixteen or so when my father died and Ma sold up and went back to live in her native Canada.

'I didn't see or hear of Fleur until a couple of years ago—at about the time of that fiasco with Katie. I was in Paris on business. I literally bumped into her on the street. She looked dreadful. She was pregnant. She was ill.

'Over dinner she told me the full story. A matter of weeks after my father's death Fleur had run away from home. She made a living of sorts singing in bars, then she got a job in a nightclub and things began to look up for her. Then came a brief spell of success. She made a record that shot to the top of the charts, but neither of her adoptive parents had lived to see her succeed, and that success turned sour because she became pregnant and within weeks of that she endured two blows—either one of which would have knocked the stuffing out of most other people.

'Her lover dropped her. He disowned the coming baby. He was already married and aiming to go into

politics. The second blow was mortal. Literally. She
was diagnosed as suffering from a terminal illness and
the prognosis was bleak. She could carry the child to
term but she wouldn't survive the birth for more than
a few weeks. She was alone, she was pregnant, she
knew she was dying.'

'So you married her.' Caro didn't have to be told.
It was the sort of thing he would do.

'It was the only thing to do. We made sure she
looked fabulous in her wedding photographs. She was
going out while she was still at the top; she couldn't
bear anyone to know her pathetic story. We announced her pregnancy and her temporary retirement
from the music scene and went to earth in Canada
where we stayed with Ma. When Sophie was born I
adopted her, and between that and the security of
those few months of stability within marriage I believe her last weeks were as contented as they could
be in the circumstances.'

Caro felt almost too emotional to speak. But she
managed, 'That is so sad—I think I'm going to cry!'

'Don't.' He cupped her face between his hands
again. 'The last thing Fleur would have wanted was
for anyone to be sad on her account. She was courageous and cheerful. And I mean always. We often
talked about the future, what she wanted for
Sophie—and the thing she wanted most of all was for
me to marry again, to give Sophie a mother as well
as a father. ''And next time make sure you marry for
love!'' she used to say. So don't be sad, my darling.'

This man of hers was a thorough-going hero. Caro
wound her arms around his neck and kissed him
fiercely.

'Does that mean you're happy to be the second Mrs Helliar?' Finn asked, long minutes later, his breathing ragged, his heart trying to pump its way out of his chest.

'More than happy. Ecstatic. Oh, Finn,' she breathed. 'Kiss me again. Don't start something you've no intention of finishing!'

'I have every intention of reaching a conclusion satisfactory to all parties.' He unwound her arms from around his neck, slid out of the door, helped her down and lifted her into his arms. 'But not out here. Why else did I lay on champagne and a bed?'

He began to carry her towards the door of their future home, the grazing of his lips on hers, the steady beat of his heart against hers a promise of loving to come, a loving that would stay with them until the end of time.

EPILOGUE

'MRS HELLIAR, has anyone ever told you how adorable you are?'

As he sat beside her on the bed, Finn's eyes were misty with love. 'Not for all of five minutes,' Caro said, leaning back against the cool linen pillows, her three-hour-old son held tenderly in her arms.

'Then I must remedy that,' he said, and did, then lifted one of her hands to his lips and kissed it softly.

This entrancing, bedazzling, fiercely loving wife of his had just presented him with a beautiful son and his heart was so full of love—for her, for the whole world—he thought it might burst.

The master bedroom at Mytton Wells was cooler now, long gauzy curtains moving idly in the breeze at the open windows. It had been another long, hot, wonderful summer. And for the first time in what seemed like days but which had been, apparently, only a few short hours they had the room to themselves, the midwives finally having departed with instructions to ask his mother—who had flown over from Canada two weeks ago to be sure to be on hand for the birth of her grandchild—to bring Sophie up to meet her baby brother in fifteen minutes.

He hadn't been too happy about the idea of a home birth, but everything had been fine and he was glad it had happened this way. Caro had been right in this, just as she had been right when shortly after their marriage she'd announced her intention of training Honor up to take her place at the agency because she was too happy to spend her time wandering, in theory, around the edges of other people's families. She wanted to concentrate, full-time, and hands very definitely on, on her own.

And she was doing a brilliant job.

'You don't think Sophie will feel jealous?' Caro's fingers tightened around his. 'I'd hate that.'

'Of course she won't,' Finn reassured her softly, hearing the unmistakable sounds of his daughter clomping along the polished wood floor of the passage outside the room, her excited chatter almost drowning out what he could hear of his mother's futile instructions to 'Try to go quietly, darling'.

He grinned broadly. 'That little daughter of ours is far too secure in our love and too certain of her position at the centre of our universe to be jealous of anyone or anything. Ever.'

Caro hoped he was right. No matter how many children she ended up having, and how deeply and devotedly she loved them all, Sophie would always have a special place in her heart. She practically held her breath as the sturdy child pushed through the partially open door and walked importantly over to the king-size bed.

At two years and a bit Sophie Helliar was an assured young lady. Her grandmother had dressed her in her best sprigged cotton dress and brushed her golden curls until they positively glittered. But she was dragging the battered old toy rabbit behind her and Caro's heart sank as Lucy announced, 'She would bring that old thing with her!' then stood at the foot of the bed and smiled mistily at her young family.

As if he knew what she was thinking—that Sophie always took the squashy, lop-eared blue velvet rabbit to bed and was feeling too insecure to do without it in the daytime now—Finn gave Caro's hand a re-assuring squeeze and asked his daughter, 'Well, and what do you think of him? His name is Luke. Come and be introduced.'

Sophie said nothing until she'd clambered up onto the bed and settled herself between her parents. She stared intently at the new arrival, kissed him soundly then laid the battered, squashy rabbit on top of him and announced, 'The brother can have Horn to sleep in his bed. Horn will make him feel comfy.'

'Thank you, sweetheart,' Caro said in a wobbly voice. 'That is very thoughtful of you.' And Finn, circling the three most precious people in his world with his loving arms, knew that there was too much love around for anyone, ever, to do anything other than wallow in a glorious surfeit of the stuff.

Take 4 bestselling love stories FREE

Plus get a FREE surprise gift!

Presents Extravaganza

25 YEARS!

Harlequin Presents® will make it even
easier to pick up a Presents title—
and you'll be glad you did!

As an added bonus you can save
$1.00 off the purchase of your next
Harlequin Presents® book!

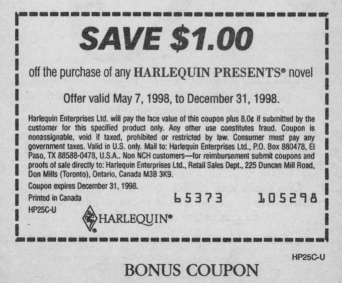

SAVE $1.00

off the purchase of any **HARLEQUIN PRESENTS**® novel

Offer valid May 7, 1998, to December 31, 1998.

HP25C-U

BONUS COUPON

Presents Extravaganza
25 YEARS!

With the purchase of two Harlequin Presents® books, you can send in for a FREE Silvertone Book Pendant. Retail value $19.95. It's our gift to you!

FREE SILVERTONE BOOK PENDANT

On the official proof-of-purchase coupon below, fill in your name, address and zip or postal code, and send it, plus $1.50 U.S./ $2.50 CAN. for postage and handling, (check or money order—please do not send cash), to Harlequin books: In the U.S.: 3010 Walden Avenue, P.O. Box 9077, Buffalo, N.Y. 14269-9077; In Canada: P.O. Box 609, Fort Erie, Ontario L2A 5X3. Please allow 4-6 weeks for delivery. Order your Silvertone Book Pendant now! Quantities are limited. Offer for the FREE Silvertone Book Pendant expires December 31, 1998.

Harlequin Presents®
Extravaganza!

Official Proof of Purchase
"Please send me a FREE Silvertone Book Pendant."

Name: _____

Address: _____

City: _____

State/Prov.: _____ Zip/Postal Code: _____

Reader Service Account: _____

◆ HARLEQUIN®

097 KGP CSAY 716-1

HP25POP

Coming Next Month

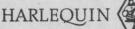 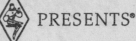

THE BEST HAS JUST GOTTEN BETTER!

#1959 SINFUL PLEASURES Anne Mather
Megan was back in San Felipe to find that much had changed.
Her stepsister's son, Remy, had been nine to her fifteen when
she saw him last—now he was a deeply attractive man. And
Megan sensed danger.

#1960 THE MARRIAGE CAMPAIGN Helen Bianchin
Dominic wanted Francesca, and he'd planned a very special
campaign for winning her. She may be wary of loving again,
but he was going to pursue, charm and seduce her
relentlessly—until she said yes!

#1961 THE SECRET WIFE Lynne Graham
Nothing could have prepared Rosie for Greek tycoon
Constantine Voulos—or his insistence that she marry him! But
she soon realized she couldn't just be his temporary wife. Her
secret would have to be told!

#1962 THE DIVORCÉE SAID YES! Sandra Marton
(The Wedding of the Year)
When Chase suggested to ex-wife, Annie, that they pretend to
get back together to reassure their daughter that love could
last, Annie was amazed. But then she found herself agreeing
to his plan....

#1963 ULTIMATE TEMPTATION Sara Craven
(Nanny Wanted!)
Count Giulio Falcone needed a nanny to look after his sister's
children. Lucy was in his debt *and* in his house. Suddenly she
found herself in the wrong place at the wrong time, with the
ultimate temptation—Giulio!

#1964 GIRL TROUBLE Sandra Field
(Man Talk)
Cade loved Lori, but she had two daughters—one of whom
had taken an instant dislike to him. He only wanted one
blonde in his life, not three. Trouble was, getting Lori into his
bed meant accepting the little girls into his heart!